'As Turner's memories are unlocked, so are his feelings — and his language…Although he went out to find a killer, Turner earns his redemption by finding his own lost voice.'
– *New York Times*

'features another complex protagonist and a story brimming with Southern atmosphere…*Cypress Grove* should attract an even broader audience for [Sallis'] visually tantalizing, astute observations on crime and the human condition'
– *Los Angeles Times*

'Sallis is a fastidious man, intelligent and widely read. There's nothing slapdash or merely strategic about his work … peculiar and visionary'
– *London Review of Books*

'This compelling book is beautifully written. It flows naturally off the pages like a lazy Southern river on a hot, steamy summer's night … Its style, story-telling, psychological elements, are all masterful… a book to be savoured'
– *Mystery Review*

'Sallis, a poet in private eye's clothing, has found in Turner a rich new character to hang around with. Let's hope this isn't the last we see of him'

# Praise for James Sallis

'Sallis is an unsung genius of crime writing'
— *Independent on Sunday*

'James Sallis is a superb writer'
— *Times*

'James Sallis — he's right up there, one of the best of the best... Sallis, also a poet, is capable of smart phrasing and moments of elegiac energy'
— Ian Rankin, *Guardian*

'[A] master of America noir...Sallis creates vivid images in very few words and his taut, pared down prose is distinctive and powerful'
— *Sunday Telegraph*

'Sallis's spare, concrete prose achieves the level of poetry'
— *Telegraph*

'Sallis is a wonderful writer, dark, lyrical and compelling'
— *Spectator*

'Unlike those pretenders who play in dark alleys and think they're tough, James Sallis writes from an authentic noir sensibility, a state of mind that hovers between amoral indifference and profound existential despair'
— *New York Times*

'Carefully crafted, restrained and eloquent'
– *Times Literary Supplement*

'James Sallis is without doubt the most underrated novelist currently working in America'
– *Catholic Herald*

'Sallis writes crime novels that read like literature'
– *Los Angeles Times*

# SELECTED WORKS BY JAMES SALLIS

## Novels Published by No Exit Press

## Other Novels

## Stories

## Poems

*Sorrow's Kitchen*
*My Tongue In Other Cheeks: Selected Translations*

## As Editor

*Ash of Stars: On the Writing of Samuel R. Delany*
*Jazz Guitars*
*The Guitar In Jazz*

## Other

*The Guitar Players*
*Difficult Lives*
*Saint Glinglin by Raymond Queneau* (translator)
*Chester Himes: A Life*
*A James Sallis Reader*

# CYPRESS GROVE

## Turner Trilogy Book One

## JAMES SALLIS

**25 years**
**NO EXIT**

This edition published in 2012
by No Exit Press, an imprint of
Oldcastle Books Ltd,
PO Box 394,
Harpenden,
Herts, AL5 1XJ

www.noexit.co.uk

A CIP catalogue record for this book is available from the British Library

This is a work of fiction. Names, characters, places, and incidents either are
the product of the author's imagination, or are used fictitiously, and any
resemblance to actual persons, living or dead, businesses, companies, events or
locales is entirely coincidental

ISBNs
978-1-84243-728-5 Paperback
978-1-84243-729-2 kindle
978-1-84243-730-8 epub
978-1-84243-731-5 pdf

2 4 6 8 10 9 7 5 3 1

Typeset by Avocet Typeset, Chilton, Aylesbury, Bucks
in 11.5 on 14.5pt Bembo
Printed and bound by CPI Group (UK) Ltd, Croydon, CR0 4YY

**For further information about Crime Fiction
visit crimetime.co.uk / @crimetimeuk**

To the memory of

# DAMON KNIGHT

*Great man,*
*great friend,*
*greatly missed*

*My thanks to George Gibson and Michael Seidman*
*for their patience and persistent support;*

*to Vicky, as always;*

*and to Major Mark Collins*
*of the Memphis Police Department.*

If your kneebone achin'
and your body cold ...
You just gettin' ready, honey,
for the cypress grove.

—*Skip James, "Cypress Grove Blues"*

# Chapter One

I HEARD THE JEEP A HALF MILE OFF. It came up around the lake, and when it hit the bend, birds took flight. They boiled up out of the trees, straight up, then, as though heavy wind had caught them, veered abruptly, all at once, sharp right. Most of those trees had been standing forty or fifty years. Most of the birds had been around less than a year and wouldn't be around much longer. I was somewhere in between.

I watched the Jeep as it emerged from trees and the driver dropped into third for the glide down that long incline to the cabin. Afternoon light on the lake turned it to tinfoil. Not much sound. High-in-the-throat hum of the well-maintained engine. From time to time the rustle of dry leaves as wind struck them and they tried to ring like bells there on the trees.

He pulled up a few yards distant, under the pecan tree. Shells on its yield so hard you had to stomp them to get to half a spoonful of meat. I swore that squirrels left them lined up under tires for cracking and sat alongside waiting. He got out of the Jeep and stood beside it. Wearing gray work clothes from Sears, old-fashioned wide-top Wellingtons and what looked to be an expensive hat, though one that would have been more at home further south and west. He stood leaning back against the driver's door with arms crossed, looking around. Folks around here don't move fast. They grow up respecting other folks' homes, their land and privacy, whatever lines have been drawn, some of them invisible. Respecting the history of the place, too. They sidle up, as they say; ease into things. Maybe that's why I was here.

"Good afternoon," he said, final syllable turned up slightly in such a way that his utterance might be taken as observation, greeting, query.

"They all are."

He nodded. "There is that. Even the worst of them, here in God's country... Not interrupting anything, I hope."

I shook my head.

"Good. That's good." He pushed himself off the door, turned to reach inside, came out with a paper sack. "Looks to be room for the both of us up there on that porch."

I waved him aboard. Settling into the other chair, like my own a straightback kitchen chair gone rickety and braced with crisscrosses of sisal twine, he passed across the sack.

"Brought this."

I skinned paper back to a bottle of Wild Turkey.

"Talk to Nathan, by some chance?"

My visitor nodded. "He said, as the two of us hadn't met before, it might be a good idea to bring along a little something. Grease the wheels."

Nathan'd lived in a cabin up here for sixty years or more. Step on his land, whoever you were, you'd get greeted with a volley of buckshot; that's what everyone said. But not long after I moved in, Nathan started turning up with a bottle every few weeks and we'd sit out here on the porch or, coolish days, inside by the fire, passing the bottle wordlessly back and forth till it was gone.

I went in to get glasses. Poured us both tall soldiers and handed his across. He held it up to the light, sipped, sighed.

"Been meaning to get up this way and say hello," he said. "Things keep shouldering in, though. I figured it could wait. Not like either of us was going anywhere."

That was it for some time. We sat watching squirrels climb trees and leap between them. I'd nailed an old rusted pan onto the pecan tree and kept it filled with pecans for them. From time to time one or the other of us reached out to pour a freshener. Nothing much else moved. Up here you're never far away from knowing that time's an illusion, a lie.

We were into the last couple of inches of the bottle when he spoke again.

"Hunt?"

I shook my head. "Did my share of it as a boy. I think that may have been the only thing my old man loved. Game on the table most days. Deer, rabbit, squirrel, quail and dove, be begging people to take some. He never used anything but a .22."

"Gone now?"

"When I was twelve."

"Mine too."

I went in and made coffee, heated up stew from a couple of days back. When I returned to the porch with two bowls, dark'd gone halfway up the trees and the sounds around us had changed. Insects throbbed and thrummed. Frogs down by the lake sang out with that hollow, aching sound they have.

"Coffee to follow," I told him. "Unless you want it now."

"After's fine."

We sat over our stew. I'd balanced a thick slab of bread on each bowl, for dunking. Since I'd baked the bread almost a week before and it was going hard on stale, that worked just fine. So for a time we spooned, slurped, dunked and licked. Dribbles ran down shirtfronts and chins. I took in the bowls, brought out coffee.

"Never been much inclined to pry into a man's business."

Steam from the cups rose about our faces.

"Why you're here, where you're from, all that. Folks do pay me to keep track of what's going on in these parts, though. Like a lot of things in life, striking a balance's the secret to it."

Frogs had given up. Paired by now. Shut out by darkness. Resigned to spending their evening or life alone. Time for mosquitoes to take over, and they swarmed about us. I went in to replenish our coffee and, returning, told him, "No great secret to it. I was a cop. Spent eleven years in prison. Spent a few more years as a productive citizen. Then retired and came here. No reason things have to get more complicated than that."

He nodded. "Always do, though. It's in our nature."

I watched as a mosquito lit on the back of my hand, squatted a moment and flew away. A machine, really. Uncomplicated. Designed and set in motion to perform its single function perfectly.

"Can I do something for you, Sheriff?"

He held up his cup. "Great coffee."

"Bring a pot of water to boil, take it off the fire and throw in coffee. Cover and let sit."

"That simple."

I nodded.

He took another sip and looked about. "Peaceful out here, isn't it?"

"Not really."

An owl flew by, feet and tail of its prey, a rodent of some sort, dangling.

"Tell the truth, I kind of hoped I might be able to persuade you to help me. With a murder."

# Chapter Two

LIFE, SOMEONE SAID, IS WHAT HAPPENS while we're waiting around for other things to happen that never do.

*Amen!* as Brother Douglas would have said, hoisting his Bible like a sword and brandishing it there framed by stained-glass windows depicting the Parable of the Talents, Mary Magdalene at the tomb, the Assumption.

Back then and back home, there among kudzu in the westward cup of Crowley's Ridge and eastward levees built to keep the river out, I'd been a golden child, headed for greatness—greatness meaning only escape from that town and its mean horizons. I'd ridden the cockhorse of a scholarship down the river to New Orleans, then back up it to Chicago (following the course of jazz) where, once I had secured a fellowship, head and future pointed like twin bullets towards professordom. Then our President went surreptitiously to war and took me with him. Walking on elbows through green even greener than that I'd grown up among, I recited Chaucer, recalled Euclid, enumerated, as a means of staying awake and alert, principles of economy— and left them there behind me on the trail: spore, droppings.

No difficulty for *this* boy, rejoining society. I got off the plane on a Friday, in Memphis, stood outside the bus station for an hour or so without going inside, then left. Never made it home. Found a cheap hotel. Monday I walked halfway across the city to the PD and filled out an application. Why the PD? After all these years, I can't remember any particular train of thought that led me there. I'd spent two and a half years getting shot at. Maybe I figured that was qualification enough.

Weeks later, instead of walking on elbows, I was sitting in a Ford that swayed and bucked like a son of a bitch, cylinders banging the whole time. Still making my way through the wilderness, though. If anything, the city was a stranger, more alien place to me than the jungle had been. Officer Billy Nabors was driving. He had breath that would peel paint and paper off walls and singe the pinfeathers off chickens.

"What I need you to do," he said, "is just shut the fuck up and sit there and keep your eyes open. Till I tell you to do something else, that's *all* I need you to do."

He hauled the beast down Jefferson towards Washington Bottoms, over a spectacular collection of potholes and into what appeared to be either a long-abandoned warehouse district or the set for some postwar science fiction epic. We pulled up alongside the only visible life-forms hereabouts, all of them hovering about a Spur station advertising "Best Barbecue." A four-floor apartment house across the street had fallen into itself and a young woman sat on the curb outside staring at her shoes, strings of saliva snailing slowly down a black T-shirt reading ATEFUL DE D. A huge rotting wooden tooth hung outside the onetime dentist's office to the right. The empty lot to the left had grown a fine crop of treadbare auto tires, bags of garbage, bits and pieces of shopping carts, bicycles and plastic coolers, jagged chunks of brick and cinder block.

Nabors had the special on a kaiser roll, Fritos and a 20-ounce coffee. I copied the coffee, passed on the rest. Hell, I could live for a week off what he spilled down his shirtfront. But that day his shirt was destined to stay clean a while longer, because, once we'd settled back in the squad and he started unwrapping, we got a call. Disturbance of the peace, Magnolia Arms, apartment 24.

He drove us twelve blocks to a place that looked pretty much like the one we'd left.

"Gotta be your first DP, right?"

I nodded.

"Shit." He looked down at his wrapped barbeque. Grease crept out slowly onto the dash. "You sit here. Anything looks out of whack, you hear anything, you call in Officer Needs Assistance. Don't think about it, don't try to figure it out, just hit the fuckin' button. You got that?"

"Gee, I'm not sure, Cap'n. You know how I is."

Nabors rolled his eyes. "What the fuck'd I do? Just what the fuck'd I do?"

Opening the door, he pulled himself out and struggled up plank-and-pipe stairs. I watched him make his way along the second tier. Intent, focused. I reached over and got his fucking sandwich and threw it out the window. He knocked at 24. Stood there a moment talking, then went in. The door closed.

The door closed, and nothing else happened. There were lights on inside. Nothing else happened for a long time. I got out of the squad, went around to the back. Following some revisionist ordinance, a cheap, ill-fitting fire escape had been tacked on. I pulled at the rung, saw landings go swaying above, bolts about to let go. Started up, thinking about all those movies with suspension bridges.

I'd made it to the window of 24 and was reaching to try it when a gunshot brought me around. I kicked the window in and went after it.

Through the bathroom door I saw Nabors on the floor. No idea how badly he might have been hurt. Gun dangling, a young Hispanic stood over him. He looked up at me, nose running, eyes blank as two halves of a pecan shell. Like guys too long in a country that had just shut down, because that was the only way they could make it.

I shot him.

It all happened in maybe twenty seconds, and for years afterward, in memory, I'd count it out, one thousand, two thousand… At the time, it seemed to go on forever, especially that last moment, with him sitting there slumped against the wall and me standing with my S&W .38 still extended. Right hand only, not the officially taught and approved grip, never sighting but firing by instinct, how I'd learned to shoot back home and the only way that ever worked for me.

I'd hit him an inch or so off the center of his chest. For a moment as I bent above him, there was a whistling sound and frothy blood bubbling up out of the amazingly small wound, before everything stopped. He had three crucifixes looped around his neck, a tattoo of barbed wire beneath.

Nabors lay there lamenting the loss of his barbeque. Man like him, that's the note he should go out on. But he wasn't going out, not this time. I picked up the phone and called in Officer Down and location. Only then did it occur to me that I hadn't cleared the rest of the apartment.

Not much rest to clear, as it happened. A reeking bathroom, a hallway with indoor-outdoor carpeting frayed like buckskin at the edges. Boxes sat everywhere, most of them unpacked, others torn open and dug through, contents spilling half out. The girl was in the back bedroom, in a closet, arms lashed to the crossbar, feet looped about with clothesline threaded into stacked cinder blocks. Her breasts hung sadly, blood trickled down her thighs, and her eyes were bright. She was fourteen.

# Chapter Three

"I'M IN OVER MY HEAD," Sheriff Bates said. "You came up around here, right?"

"Close enough."

"Then you know how it is."

We were in his Jeep, heading back towards town. Dirt roads pitted as a teenager's face. Now we turned out of the trees onto worn blacktop. The radio mounted beneath his dash crackled.

"Weekends, we break up bar fights, haul in drunk drivers. Maybe kids pay someone to buy them a case of beer and party till they get to be a nuisance, or some guy down on his luck climbs in a window and comes back out with a pillowcase full of flatware, prescription drugs, a laptop or TV. Not like there's much anywhere he can *go* with it. Once in a blue moon a husband slaps his wife down once too often, gets a butcher knife planted in his shoulder or a frypan laid up alongside his head."

The radio crackled again. Didn't sound to me any different from previous crackles, but Bates picked up the mike. "I'm on my way in."

"Ten-four." Guy at the other end loved those vowels, rolled them around in his mouth like marbles.

Bates hung the mike back on its stirrup.

"Don Lee. You'll be meeting him here shortly. Eager to get home to his six-pack and his new wife, most likely in that order. What time's it got to be, anyway?"

"Little after eight."

"My month to cover nights. Natural order of things, Don Lee'd be gone hours ago. Lisa'd have had his meat and potatoes on the table, he'd be on the couch and his second beer while she washed up. But long as I'm out of pocket, he's stuck there."

Bates hauled the Jeep hard right and we skidded out onto what passes for a highway around here, picking up speed. Almost immediately, though, he geared down, braked.

"You need help there, Ida?"

A saddle-oxford Buick, cream over blue, vintage circa '48, sat steaming in the right lane. An elderly woman all in white, vintage a couple of decades prior, stood alongside. She wore a hat that made you want to hide Easter eggs in it.

"Course not. Just have to let it cool down, same as always."

"I figured. You say hi to Karl for me, now."

"I'll say it. What he hears …"

A mile or so further along, the sheriff said, "Back in Memphis you had the highest clearance rate on homicides of anyone on the force."

"You've done your homework."

"I'm not in a habit of drafting help. Tend to be cautious about it."

"Then you know it wasn't me, it was us. What part wasn't plain luck owes mostly to my partner. I'd be jumping hoops of intuition, flying high. Meanwhile he was back down there on the ground thinking things methodically through."

"That would be Randy—right?"

I nodded.

"Like I said, I'm in over my head. Expertise, luck, intuition—we'll take whatever you've got."

We came in from the north, onto deserted streets. Pop. 1280, a sign said. Passed Jay's Diner with its scatter of cars and trucks outside, drugstore and hardware store gone dark, A&P, Dollar $tore, Baptist church, Gulf station. Pulled in behind city hall. One-story prefab painted gray. Probably took them all of a week to put it up, and it'd be there forever, long as the glue held. The paint job was recent and hurried, with a light frosting of gray on bushes alongside. A single black-and-white sat nosed in close outside. Inside, a rangy man in polyester doing its best to look like khaki sat nosed close to the desk. On it were a radio, a ten-year-old Apple computer and a stack of magazines, one of which he was paging through. He looked up as we came in. Wet brown eyes that reminded me of spaniels, ruddy face narrow and shallow like a shovel, thin hair. Something electric about him, though. Sparks and small connections jumping around in there unremarked.

"Anything going on?" Bates said.

"'Bout what you'd expect. Couple of minor accidents at getting-off time. Old Lady Siler reported her purse stolen, then remembered she'd locked it in the trunk of her car. I ran the spare key out, as usual. Jimmy Allen showed up at his wife's house around dark and started pounding on the door. Then he tried to steal the car. When I got there, he had two

23

wires pulled down out of the radio, trying to hotwire them."

"Been at it for an hour or more, if I know Jimmy."

"Prob'ly so."

"He in back?"

"Out flat."

"This goes on, Jimmy might as well just start having his mail delivered here."

Bates walked over and closed three of the four light switches on the panel by the door. Much of the room fell gray, leaving us and desk in a pool of dim light outside which shadows jumped and slid.

"Don Lee, this's Mr. Turner."

The deputy held out a hard, lean hand and I took it. A good handshake, no show to it, just what it was. Like the man, I suspected.

"Pleased to have you, Detective."

"Just Turner. I haven't been a detective for a long time."

"Hope you're not telling us you forget how," Bates said.

"No. What happens is, you stop believing it matters."

"And does it?" This from Don Lee.

"Does it matter, or does it stop?"

"There's a difference?"

In that instant I knew I liked him. Liked them both. All I'd wanted was to be left alone, and I'd taken giant steps to ensure that. Rarely strayed far from the cabin, had goods delivered monthly. The last thing I'd wanted was ever again to be part of an investigation, to have to go rummaging through other people's lives, messes and misdemeanors, other people's madnesses, other people's minds.

"Why don't you fill me in?" I said.

"You'n go on home," Bates told his deputy. "Appreciate

your holding down the fort. Dinner must be getting colder by the minute."

"All the same to you, I'd as soon stay," Don Lee said.

# Chapter Four

NABORS MADE IT, SURVIVED THE SHOOTING that is, but he never came back on active duty. Mondays, my day off, I visited him at the rehab facility out in Whitehaven. Sculptured, impossibly green lawns with sprinklers that went off like miniature Old Faithfuls, squat ugly buildings. Never did figure what those were made of, but they put me in mind of Legos. Soft-handed young doctors and platoons of coiffured, elegantly eyelashed young nurses manning the pressure locks, all of them with mouthfuls of comfort like mush for both visitors and patients, couldn't spit out those lumps of good advice fast enough.

Suddenly around the station house everyone knew who I was. Older cops who'd pointedly ignored me before, smelling as they often did of sweat socks, stale bourbon or beer, aftershave and last night's whore, now nodded to me in the locker room. Two shifts in a row I got put in a squad that didn't haul hard left or need new tires and assigned uptown. Really knew I was some kind of made man the day Fishbelly Joe, the blind albino who'd run a hot dog stand outside the station house as long as anyone could remember, refused my money.

Then one Monday afternoon as I reported for the 3–11, word surfaced from the Captain. Come see him.

"I think it's a mistake, Turner," he said. "You're not ready for it. But you're bumped to detective."

I'd been a cop, what, two or three months at that point? Most of the men I worked with were ten, twenty years older, and most of them had packed their lives into the work. Little wonder they'd been reluctant to accept me, and only began to do so, haltingly, now.

Did I for even a moment recognize this as a repeat of what happened in the service? No. (But how could I not have?) There I'd passed from basic training to special forces in a matter of weeks, as in one of those TV shows where events stumble over one another trying to get past. I'm a quick study, have a quirky mind that gets on to things instantly. While others are still floundering and doing belly flops, I'm walking around, looking good—but my understanding never extends far beneath the surface.

At that time, remember, I had little enough training to speak of, and almost no experience. And the fact that Nabors and I had violated procedure was something I just couldn't get my head around. That went on every moment of every shift of every day, sure. No one did things by the book. You cut corners, jury-rigged, improvised, faked it, got by. But few of those shortcuts ended up with a fatal shooting and a seasoned officer going down. I kept ticking off the mistakes in my head.

We were supposed to stay together at all times. We should both have responded.

When I began to suspect that something had gone badly south, I'd started in without calling for backup.

I'd failed to follow my senior partner's orders.

Then, failing also to identify myself or fire a warning shot (which back then, before *Garner v. Tennessee,* remained policy), I'd shot a man dead.

Interestingly enough, few questions got asked outside my own head, and none of this ever came up for any sort of review. But right after gypsies and sailors, cops are the most superstitious folk alive, and while I was newly on the list of good guys, looked up to in some weird, abstract fashion, the whole thing stayed weird: no one wanted to partner with me.

So for a time, in direct violation of department policy, I rode by myself in the best cars the department had to offer. Ranked detective, I still spent most of my shift on routine calls.

What happened next I'm still not clear on, but somewhere (arbitrarily, I assume, from my experience with bureaucracies pre and post) a decision was made, and I started finding myself beside guys no one else would put up with. Likes attracting? Or maybe they were there as department brass's last, desperate effort to shake them out of the tree. We're talking rookies too dumb for Gilligan's island here, lawmen Andy wouldn't let have *one* bullet, bullies fresh off the schoolyard, lumbering southern gentlemen who stood when ladies and elders entered the room but had screenings of *Shane* and *The Ox-Bow Incident* playing continuously in their heads.

Then one morning I looked to the right, or so it seemed, and Gardner was sitting there. We'd just come off an unwarranted noise call, I'd let him handle it, and the boy'd done good.

What you got to do is put on their lives, way you do a robe or an old shirt, he told me. You stand outside looking, no way you can see in, no way they're gonna trust you.

That what they teach you these days?

Right after the choke hold, he said.

We'd been riding together three or four months by then. Why was he any different from the others? I'm not sure he was. Could have been me: maybe I'd just come around to the point where I was ready to start forging connections again. Or maybe it was just that the son of a bitch wouldn't give up. I'd done everything I could do to ignore him, frustrate him, demean him, and he just sat there sipping coffee and smiling, asking what I wanted for lunch. While I was busily turning into Nabors.

Like myself, Gardner came up from the backlands. But whereas I loved cities and needed them, or thought I did, he'd never caught on to city ways. Part of him would always be walking down some dirt road along train tracks, stopping by the bait shop for a cold drink. He was a good, simple man.

One morning over coffee Gardner told me he was quitting. His girl back home had written to tell him she was pregnant. He went, found out soon enough that she wasn't pregnant at all, only lonely, and shortly after turned up in Memphis again. Teamed with someone else now, but we kept in touch. After that, his heart never quite let him get back into the job. Riding alone one night, he answered a disturbance call at a motel, an altercation between a prostitute name L'il Sal and her client. All of us knew L'il Sal. She'd turn black to white and charm the sun down if it gave her points. Either Gardner had forgotten L'il Sal or didn't care. He was listening to her story when the john came up behind and slit his throat with a buck knife.

# Chapter Five

"ORDINARILY, THE WAY WE'D WORK this is, State would send someone over. Highway Patrol. But they're too shorthanded, couple of guys out on short-term disability, another off in Virginia for training. Not to mention the backup in their own cases. Someone'll be there, the barracks commander told me, but when he'll be there ..." Bates grunted. "I also got the notion he might not be the barrack's best."

"That had to make you feel better."

"You bet it did. We still get breakfast, Thelma?" he said to the waitress who'd dropped off coffees, gone about her business and now ambled back around to us. She wore badly pilled gray polyester slacks, a black sweater hanging down almost to her knees in front and hiked over her butt behind. Hair pinned up in a loose swirl from which strands had escaped and hung out like insect legs.

"You see there on the menu where it says breakfast twenty-four hours a day, Lonnie?"

"You're not open twenty-four hours a day, Thelma."

"Not much gets by you, does it? Must be what keeps down the criminal element hereabouts, why the good people of this town keep reelecting you."

"What's good?"

"Nothing. But you can eat most of it."

I found myself wondering how many times they'd been through this routine.

"What are you doing asking me anyway? We both know what you're gonna have. Three eggs over easy, grits, ham. You're done, some of these other folk might appreciate getting the chance to order."

"Got it by yourself, huh?"

"Yeah. You want anything besides coffee, Don Lee?"

"Coffee'll do me," he said.

"New girl supposed to be here, worked half a shift yesterday. Guess she decided maybe this wasn't what she wanted to do with her life after all. Her loss. God knows there's rewards. Toast?"

Sheriff Bates nodded.

"You know what, I'll have an order of toast, too," Don Lee said.

"Been most of an hour since the boy ate," Bates said.

"And what can I get you, sir?"

I ordered a club sandwich on wheat without mayo and a salad, no dressing. The coffee was actually very good. For a long time I'd never order coffee in restaurants. I liked it the way we used to fix it back home, throwing a handful of coffee into boiling water. Nothing else ever seemed worth bothering with. Then coffeehouses started sprouting everywhere. I didn't much care for their little ribbon-tied bundles of gourmet this and that, trinkets and dumb posters, but they brought coffee in America to a new level.

"What do you want to know?" Bates said.

"Usually I find it doesn't much matter what I want to know, I just get what people want to tell me. So I go with that." I looked around. A dozen or so people were in the diner, most of them sitting alone over plates of chicken-fried steaks, burgers, spaghetti. Three middle-aged women at a back table laughing too loudly and looking about furtively to see if anyone noticed. "It's been a while, as I said. But as I recall, we generally started with a body."

"And while we do things our own way up here, we don't do them *that* differently." Bates smiled. "Don Lee was on duty that night."

Caught by surprise, the deputy said, "Right," then took a sip of coffee to gather himself. "Call came in a little after twelve, which is when the bars close 'round here—"

"What day was it?"

"Beg pardon?"

"I'm assuming it had to be a weekday, that bars don't close at twelve on weekends even 'round here."

"Right. It was a Monday."

"Back in Memphis everyone called Monday the day nothing ever happens."

"Hard to tell it from any other day 'round here."

"You were on by yourself, right? There're only the two of you?"

"Lonnie and me, right. We have someone on dispatch, on the radio that is, eight to four every day. Lonnie's daughter, mostly, or else Danny Lambert. He was sheriff close to twenty years before retiring. And we get lots of part-time help with answering phones, filing, all that, from Smith High. Secretarial classes looking for … what do they call them?"

"Practicums," Bates said.

"Right."

"Look," I said. "I don't want to come on like some kind of asshole here." Maybe I was bearing down too hard. "You two've worked together a while, you have a pace of your own. So does the town. Out of habit, experience, just because I'm who I am, I'm inclined to go about this a certain way. But it's your investigation—yours all the way. I'm a ride-along."

"Appreciate your saying that," Bates said. "But we'd be more than one kind of fool not to accept the very assistance we asked for."

"Okay… So how'd the call come?" I asked.

Don Lee answered. "Kids phoned it in, out there looking for a place to park. They'll go out to a block of new houses— every few years developers put these up, but no one ever seems to move into them—and they'll back in a driveway like they belong there. Girl stops with bra at half-mast. What's wrong? Seth says. Seth McEvoy. Quarterback with the high school team, plays clarinet, honor student. What *is* that? Sarah says. Sarah Perkins, her family runs the local dollar store. Sarah herself's a few steps off to the side of most of us, I guess. At any rate, she points."

Our food came. Thelma dealt plates off an extended arm, stepped away and came back with a tray holding A-1 steak sauce, Tabasco, ketchup, Worcestershire. Seeing it, I had a rush of recognition. If we ordered iced tea, she'd ask sweetened or unsweetened.

"Y'all set, then?"

"Looks great, Thelma. Thanks."

"What she was pointing to was what looked like a scarecrow standing there at the side of the carport. Sarah says it moved—that was why she noticed. Doc Oldham says no way, the body'd been dead four, five days. So we figure something else moved."

"Field mice, most likely," Bates said. "We build subdivisions where they used to live, the mice don't know they're supposed to leave."

"Especially if provisions keep getting shipped in," I said.

"Right. Seth gets out of the car and goes over to look. Male, mid- to late forties, Doc figures. He's wearing two or three shirts, a pair of Wranglers so old the rivets are worn away. Been homesteading under the carport for a while from the look of it. Had a bedroll there, couple of sacks of belongings, an old backpack with one strap."

"He'd been chewed on some. Eyes and tongue, mostly."

"Postmortem?"

Don Lee nodded.

"Cause of death?"

"The developer had finished up the subdivision in a hurry and moved on. Yards still had these stakes set out in them, eighteen inches long, sharpened at one end. Someone pulled up one of those and drove it into his chest. Someone's seen one too many vampire movies, Doc said."

"That's not gonna be easy," Bates said. "Takes some industry."

"Broken fingernails," Don Lee went on, "maybe from the struggle, maybe from before, hard to say. Splinters in his palms. Tried to pull the stake out, we figure."

"Or keep it from going in."

"We found him pinned against some latticework, trellis kind of thing. Arms crossed above his head, wrists turned out. He'd been fastened up there with picture wire."

"So the body was repositioned once he was dead."

"Way it looks. Doc said the stake missed his heart but nipped the vena cava."

"Meaning it took him a while to die… Understand that I don't mean any disrespect here, but what facilities do you have for processing a crime scene?"

"State issues us kits. Back when I started, I got sent up to the capital for a couple of months, passed along what I could remember. Don Lee's studied up some on his own. We did the best we could. But like I told you up front, we're in over our heads here."

"I went back through the manual, did it all by the numbers," Don Lee told me. "Multiple photographs of the scene and the body. Bagged clothes and belongings, including a notebook—kind of a diary, I guess. Cellotaped a half-footprint I found at the edge of the carport. Took scrapings, blood samples."

I looked at Bates. He shrugged. "What can I say? Me, I blundered into this. He's meant for it."

"Thing is," Don Lee said, "I can go on scraping, photographing and logging stuff in till kingdom come, but I still just have a bunch of bags with labels on them. All potatoes, no meat."

"Where's the forensics kit now?"

"Back at the station."

"You don't usually send them through to State?"

"No *usually* to it," Bates said. "Never had occasion to use one of the things before. Fact is, we weren't even sure where we'd put them."

"State said seal it, they'd pick it up when they got here."

"No identification on the body, I'm assuming."

Binaural nods.

"And when you canvassed, showing a photo, no one knew him, no one had seen him. Just another of America's invisible men."

Yep.

I'd finished my salad and sandwich and drunk three or four cups of coffee—Thelma kept creeping up and refilling. Altogether too fine a waitress. Don Lee's toast was crumbs on a plate and four empty jam containers with tops skinned back. Clots of yolk and a pool of runny ketchup competed on the sheriff's plate.

"What I have to ask is why you're pursuing this at all. You've got a good town here. Clean, self-contained. Obviously this guy's from outside, no one's visible father, no visible mother's son. Not a single city or PD I know, whatever size, would spend an hour on this. They'd write the report, skip it over the water into the files, move right along."

"Well, they'd be used to it, of course. We're not." Bates looked to the door, where an attractive, thirtyish woman in gray suit and lacy off-white blouse stood looking back. "Tell me that's not our State guy."

"That's not our State guy," Don Lee said.

"You know damn well it is."

As though to confirm, she strode towards us.

"We don't trip over bodies too often 'round here," Don Lee said.

"And when we do"—this from Bates—"they don't usually have the mayor's mail in their pocket."

# Chapter Six

BASICALLY THEY DON'T GET any more missing.

It wasn't a missing-persons case. In fact it was just about everything *but* a missing-persons case. Robbery, assault, murder. God knows what else. And that's the way it got passed out to us: they don't get any more missing.

The Captain himself took roll call that day. Gentlemen, he said. Officers. Has there been a misunderstanding? When I asked that you pool your efforts and give your collective best, I had expected that you would understand this was to the end of *finding* the suspect. Instead you seem collectively to have lost him.

There was laughter, uneasy laughter of a sort we all got used to over the next few months. Little by little the laughter subsided, till finally we sat stone silent through roll call. No jokes, no catcalls, none of the endless badgering that marks men thrown together in close quarters and shaky pursuits. We sat, we listened, some of us taking notes, then we rose, claimed cars, and went stolidly about our business.

It had begun long before that, of course, on a Saturday night almost two months before, when a scumbag by the name of Richards found his way into an apartment house just off campus of Memphis State where ten students lived. Most of them were out on dates. The three that weren't, he attacked. Tied them down with lamp wires and went from one to the other, back and forth. He'd come in with his member hard as a rock, one of them said, put it in her, and leave. Then after a while he'd come back. Never climaxed, or seemed to gain much pleasure from it. Lot of blood on it there at the end, one of the young women said. I kept wondering if it was my blood or someone else's, what he'd done to the others.

Richards spent his childhood in a series of foster homes, a social worker called in as consultant told us later, often shut into a room and ignored, brought food when they remembered, other times beaten or abused. My heart bled.

Anyhow, although Richards had been a busy boy, with a string of store robberies, B&Es of various sorts, auto theft and assault, rape was something new for him. But now, like a chicken-killing dog, he'd got the taste. And he liked it.

Over following weeks we got to know that campus well, spent more time there than its students did. Ants at a picnic, and just about as inconspicuous. But the next time Richards struck, it was across town, at a dorm next to Samaritan Hospital where nurses in training lived. The hospital put them up free, they attended classes half a day and helped take care of patients the rest, and after a year or so they got certified as LPNs. Women with poor and no prospects came up from all over the South. Richards went in there on a Friday evening about nine o'clock. Of the fifteen residents, eight were on duty, helping cover the evening shift as nurses although legally they weren't. Five more had gone out together for pizza and a movie. They're the ones who called it in when they got back home around midnight and found Mary Elizabeth Walker (Mobile, Alabama) and Sue Ann Simmons (Tupelo, Mississippi) strapped to their beds with duct tape. There was so much tape, one of them said, they looked like mummies, or cocoons. Mary Elizabeth stared at the wall and wouldn't respond when they spoke to her. Blood was running from both vagina and anus. Sue Simmons didn't respond either. She was dead.

We got on to Richards the usual way, through an informer. This informer lived in the neighborhood, often wound up in some of the same diners, poolrooms and bars as Richards, and almost certainly carried some grudge against him. Once we had this, still with nothing but hearsay and suspicion to take to market, we bird-dogged Richards in solid shifts, staking out his apartment from unmarked cars. For two days nothing happened. We learned a lot: that he kept unpredictable hours, had no visitors, and thrived exclusively on carry-out hamburgers. On the third day, he disappeared.

We went in with a judge's order on the fourth day and everything was just as it had been the times we'd gone in without, clothes scattered about, toiletries in place, bottle or two of prescription drugs in the bathroom, piles of mustard, salt and pepper packets on the kitchenette counter by a pool of loose change. He was gone, purely gone. Evaporated. Vanished. No one ever heard from or of him again.

That was the first one.

"A vigilante," someone said at roll call.

"The position of this department," the Captain said, "is that it's an isolated incident. That is also your position."

I'd have to pull records to check, and of course I can't, but it seems maybe two, three months went by before the next one.

These shitheads were hitting mom-and-pop stores all over the city, pistol-whipping whoever was behind the counter, mom, pop or one of numerous kids, when they objected or proved too slow at scooping up money. The perps were easy to mark. There were always three. One never spoke. He lurked on the fringes, carried a steel baseball bat over his shoulder, and moved in only when the others had got the goods and left. Then he'd swing his bat, smashing hips, knees, wrists and ankles.

Again and as usual, confidential information came up the line from one of the city's bottom feeders. Three guys who'd always had trouble putting together the price of a draft beer of late had been seen with hands wrapped around the dewy necks of imports. One of them, the informant said, was truly spooky. Never spoke, smiled a lot, sat perfectly still. Always wore a baseball cap, Yankees one day, Dodgers the next, Orioles, Rangers. Must have one hell of a collection.

Like a lot of their breed, these guys started out doing occasional hits, then, when they got away with it repeatedly, and got used to the benefits as well, started making it a regular thing. That, along with informants, is what broke most of these cases for us. Soon these guys were surfacing every Friday night.

We knew where they were staying, in a swayback, half-abandoned apartment complex out in south Memphis, near Crump and Mississippi, kind of place where plywood's been nailed up to make small rooms out of large and where to sit on the toilet you have to draw up your knees to fit them jigsawlike into the space between sink and door. But we still had to catch these guys with pants down. Every squad car went out with a list of mom-and-pop convenience stores in central Memphis that *hadn't* been hit. We circled them like sharks.

One Friday, then another, went by without these guys showing at the crib. Hadn't been around the bars either, our informant said when his contact tracked him down. No one had seen them. No one ever saw them again.

"Comes from inside the department," scuttlebutt had it in locker rooms and lounges, "who else would know."

Couple more, at least.

Someone who was offing cabdrivers. He'd hit late at night when drivers were inclined to take just about any fare they could get, he'd direct them to the city's fringes and leave them there with their heads bashed in. The department pulled hundreds of pages of copies of log sheets and dispatcher's records. We'd just begun heavy cruising of areas from which calls had come in the past when, abruptly, the killings stopped.

Next, a series of suspected arsons in upscale housing developments under construction. Two of those developments, then three, went up in flame. At the third, an elderly couple had moved in prematurely, before construction was completed. They went up in flame, too. Then it all stopped.

What the hell, the Captain said, sentiments echoed by many others, by the press, for instance, repetitively and at great length, is going on here?

We never really knew. But almost a year later, on an anonymous tip, in the woods just across the Mississippi line we found six shallow graves side by side, each topped by a wooden plaque into which had been burned a smiling skull and crossbones.

# Chapter Seven

"GET YOU SOMETHING? Coffee? Pie?"

"No thanks, Sheriff."

Introducing herself, spelling the last name, Valerie Bjorn had settled in beside Don Lee.

"You new up at State?"

"Over a year now."

"Can't help noticing you're out of uniform."

"Out of—oh. I'm not a trooper, Sheriff. I'm attorney for the barracks. Commander Bailey asked if I'd mind picking up the evidence kit."

"State's paying top dollar for messengers these days, then."

She smiled. "I live here, Sheriff. Well, not here exactly. Not far out of town, though."

"The old Ames place."

"I moved in two months ago."

"Heard someone bought it. That house's been empty a long time. Few rungs down from fixer-up would be my guess."

"I'm doing most of the work myself. My grandfather was a builder, the kind that back in his day handled everything himself, plumbing, electric, carpentry. He raised me. I started crawling under houses when I was eight or nine."

"And haven't quit yet," I said.

"I thought I had. But we're so often wrong about such things, aren't we? Not that I get much chance to crawl and so on, between my own work and what I do for the barracks. Hope you don't mind my tracking you down, Sheriff. I saw your Jeep outside."

"Not at all, Miss Bjorn."

"Val. Please."

Suddenly Thelma was at the booth, saying "Here, let me clear some room," scooping up plates and laying them along her left arm. "Get you anything else, boys? Ma'am?" Their eyes met briefly. "Some more coffee? Just made a fresh pot."

"Gettin' too late for this old man," Bates said. "Prob'ly be up through Tuesday or so, as it is."

Don Lee and I also declined.

"I'm fine," Val said. "But thank you."

"We have the check?" Bates said. Thelma turned back and shook her head. He shook his.

"How long we been doing this, Thelma? Four, five years now?"

"Sonny says I don't give you a bill. You know that."

"And you know—"

"He's my boss, Lonnie. I got to do what he tells me. That's how most of us live. What, this job isn't hard enough already?"

"Okay, okay. Anyway, your shift's almost over now."

"Life's just chockful of almosts, ain't it."

Waiting till she was gone, Bates pulled out his wallet, extracted a twenty and a five, and tucked them under the sugar bowl. Easily twice what the bill came to.

"She's dying to know who you are," he told Val.

"I got that."

"You want to come on back with me to the station, pick up that kit?"

"Would you mind if I waited and came by on my way in to work tomorrow, Sheriff? I'd dearly love to go on home now, get some rest."

"Wouldn't we all." He nodded. "What time you figure to be swinging by?"

"Seven, seven-thirty?"

"Good enough. I'm not still there, Don Lee will be."

We stood and made our way to the door.

"Goodnight, then," Val told us outside. Her eyes met each of ours in turn. She shook hands with Bates.

"Lisa's gonna hang me out to dry," Don Lee said.

"Reckon she will. Not to mention having fed your dinner to the pigs." Bates turned to me: "You'll be needing a ride back."

"You don't live in town?" Val said.

I shook my head. "Cabin up by the lake."

"Nice up there."

"It is that."

"Awfully late, though. He's one of yours, Sheriff, right?"

"Well …"

"Look, the lake's a long way. I have a spare room. Not much in there yet, an old bunk bed with a futon thrown across it, some plastic cubes, a table lamp without a table. But all that could be yours for the night."

"A kingdom."

We drove out of town in the opposite direction from the

lake, past Pappa Totzske's sprawling apple orchard and spread of seventy-five-foot chicken houses. The back seat of Val's six-year-old yellow Volvo was piled with boxes, portable files, clothing, a stack of newspapers. When she hit the key, old-time music started up at full blast. Gid Tanner, maybe. She punched the reject button on the cassette player.

"Sorry, I usually have *this* world to myself."

"Trying to assimilate?"

She laughed. "Hardly. I grew up with this, been listening to it, playing it, since I was ten years old."

"Right after you began your carpentry career."

"Exactly. Hammer, screwdriver, mandolin. Lot better with the hammer, though."

The old Ames place was six or seven miles outside town, at the end of a dirt road so deeply pitted that it could have been passed off as a child's projection map of the Grand Canyon. Papershell pecan trees and a huge, utterly wild and unkempt weeping willow stood by the house. Whole tribes could be living in the thing unbeknownst.

Val pulled up under one of the pecan trees and we climbed out. I had to hit the car door hard with the heel of my hand to get it open. She'd warned me it stuck sometimes. From the trunk she took a canvas book bag that looked to serve as briefcase. A squirrel sat on a limb just above, fussily chattering at us.

"I've only got two of the rooms really habitable so far," Val said as we entered, through the entryway into a small living room that, when the house was built, would have been used only on holidays and formal occasions. Now it sported a narrow bed, a rocking chair, a table doing triple work as desk, eating space and storage area. An antique wardrobe sat in one corner, drawers on the left in use even as the right side went on being stripped of multiple layers of varnish and paint, down to fine wood beneath. Sandpaper, a shallow dish and rags lay atop it.

On the wall by the table hung a gourd banjo. I ran my thumb across the strings, surprised to find they weren't steel but soft, like a classical guitar's.

"You really are into this."

"I guess I am."

She lifted down the banjo and, sitting, balanced it on her lap. Plucked a string or two, twisted pegs. Then started playing, back of the nail on her second finger striking a melody note then brushing other strings as the thumb popped on and off that short fifth string. "Soldier's Joy." Abruptly she stopped, putting the instrument back in place.

"Would you like tea?"

"Love it."

We went through a double doorway without doors into the kitchen.

"Here's my real bona fide as a southerner," she said.

While even the living room had about it an element of improvisation, camping out or making do, the kitchen was fully equipped, pots and provisions set out on shelves, towels on drying racks, dishes stacked in cupboards, knife block on the counter by the stove. We sat at a battered wooden table waiting for water to boil.

"Funny thing is," Val said, "I *wasn't* into this, not at all, not for a long time. As a kid I couldn't wait to get away."

"You grow up around here?"

"Kentucky. Not a spit's worth of difference. When I left for college, I swore that was it, I'd never look back. And I'd absolutely never ever *go* back. Took the two JCPenney dresses I'd worked as a waitress to buy, and some books I'd kind of forgotten to return to the library, and settled into a dorm room at Tulane. It was 1975. My Texas roommate's debut had been attended by hundreds of people. She used most of my closet space in addition to her own—I didn't need it. And those dresses looked as out of place, as anachronistic, as a gardenia in my hair."

Val poured water into a round teapot.

"I was smart. That was one of two or three ways out of there. Tulane was full of rich East Coast kids who couldn't get into Ivy League schools and poor southerners on scholarship. I lost the dresses first, the accent not long after. Most any social situation, I discovered, all you had to do was keep quiet and watch those around you. Sugar? Lemon or milk?"

I shook my head.

"By the second year you couldn't pick me out of the crowd. 'Wearing camo,' as a friend of mine put it. I finished near the top of my class, went to Baltimore as a junior partner, very junior, in a group practice."

She set a mug before me, thoughtfully turned so the chip on its lip faced away.

"I don't usually prattle on like this."

"Not a problem."

"Good." Settling back at the table, she sipped her tea. "I was up there for four years—dancing with the one who brung me, as my father would say. I liked Baltimore, the firm, liked the work. And I was good at it."

"What changed?"

"Nothing. Something. Me?" She smiled. "I wanted to,

47

anyway. Do we ever, really?"

"Change?"

Nodding.

"If we don't—if we can't—nothing else makes much sense, does it?"

She half-stood to pour us more tea. Close by, just past the window, an owl hooted.

"You're not a cop, are you?"

"Not for a long time. I was."

She waited, and after a moment I told her the basics.

"Another Cliff Notes life."

"What?"

"Those pamphlets on great books that students read instead of the books themselves. A lot of us experience our lives that way. Sum up who we are and what we're about as a few broad strokes, then do our best to cleave to it. All the good stuff, the small things and distinctions that make the rest worthwhile—Sunday mornings sitting over coffee and the paper, taste of bread fresh from the oven, the feel of wind on your skin, sensing the one you love there beside you—all these get pushed aside. Unnoticed, lost."

"If we let them."

"If we let them, right. And as much as anything else, that's why I'm here."

Dark had become absolute. Far off, frogs called. Their cries bounced across the pond behind the house, amplified by the water as though it were in fact the metal dish that moonlight made it appear. Moths beat at the window beside us, and at the kitchen's screen door.

"I drew my weapon three times," I said. God knows why I told her this. "And each time someone died. The second time, it was raining, I remember. His blood was running down the street. I was in the street too, with his head in my lap. And all the time I kept thinking: My kids are home waiting for me."

"Kids?"

"A boy and a girl. They grew up without me, have their own lives now. Probably for the best... Thing is, there in the street, in some strange way I was closer to that stranger as he died, this man I'd shot, than I've ever been to anyone else my whole life."

For some time she was silent. We both were.

"I don't know what to say."

"You don't have to say anything."

"Suddenly everything in my life seems so small."

"Our lives *are* small."

She nodded. "They are, aren't they?"

I followed her outside, onto the porch.

"Don't suppose you're hungry?"

"Not really."

"Seems I always am. Buy popcorn by the case, eat carrot sticks till I start turning orange myself and have to stop, chew celery till my teeth hurt."

We stood looking up at the sky.

"What about the third time?" she said.

"That I drew my weapon."

"Yes."

"That time, it was my own partner."

"Oh."

"There's a lot more to it," I said.

"There would be." She looked off into the trees. "Listen."

I did, and for this one perfect moment silence enveloped us, absolute silence, silence of a kind most of the world and its people have forgotten. Then the frogs started up again and from miles away the hum of cars and trucks on an interstate reached us.

# Chapter Eight

A YEAR OR SO INTO PLAYING detective, I pulled the chit on a missing-persons case. Rightfully it should have gone to Banks, who was senior and next up. But Banks was actively pursuing leads, the Lieutenant told me, on a series of abductions and rapes at local private schools. Would I mind.

A patient had disappeared from an extended-care facility. Patricia Pope, nineteen years old. She'd been out with friends celebrating her birthday with slabs of pizza and pitchers of Co'Cola. As they ferried home around eight in the evening, a drunk driver smashed head-on into their car. He'd been drinking since he got off work at five and somehow had entered the new interstate by an exit ramp. The other four in the car were killed. Patricia, riding in the front passenger seat, went through the windshield and onto the hood of the drunk's F-150. She'd received acute care in Baptist Hospital's ER, from there had been moved up to neuro ICU for several days where a shunt in her head dripped fluid into a graduated cylinder, then onto a general ward, finally to a separate, step-down facility. She made no acknowledgment when spoken to, reacted but slightly to pain. (In ER they pinched nipples and twisted. Upstairs, kinder and gentler, they poked pins about feet, ankles, forearms, torso.) Her hands had begun curling in upon themselves, first in a series of contractures pitching muscle against bone. Eyes rolled left to right continually. She was incontinent, provided nutrients through a tube that had to be reintroduced with each feeding. Caretakers threaded these tubes down her nose, blew in air through a syringe and listened with a stethoscope to be certain the tube was in her stomach.

The incident occurred on April 3. Patricia had been relocated to the EC facility on April 20. When oncoming nurses went in to check patients early in their shift on the morning of June 17, Patricia was absent from her bed. That was the way the administrator put it when he called. Absent from her bed. Like it was summer camp. The call came in at 7:06. Half an hour later, 7:38 by the brass-and-walnut clock on the wall, I was sitting in the administrator's office with a cup of venomous coffee in hand watching said administrator, Daniel Covici, MBA, CEO, rub a thumb against the burnished surface of his desk. It was the facility's desk, of course, but I had no doubt he thought of it as his own.

Most investigations are little more than paint by the numbers. You ask a string of questions in the proper order, when they don't get answered you ask them again, sooner or later you find your way to the husband or wife, spurned boy- or girlfriend, business partner, parent, younger brother, gardener, eccentric uncle, jealous neighbor. This was no different. Within the hour, down in the Human Resources basement office looking over a list of recent terminations, I came across the name of an orderly who had quit without prior notice at the end of his shift on June 16, saying simply that he was going on to another, better job. He'd been with the hospital sixteen years. Douglas Lynds. Address out by what was at that time Southwestern, a tiny freestanding wooden house.

From the street I caught glimpses of the university's Gothic spires and buttresses among the trees. The house sat ten or twelve yards back, though the frontage could scarcely be called a yard. Traces of old foundation showed, like teeth rotted to gum level. Probably there had once been a stand of such structures, housing for graduate students maybe, of which only the one remained. It was in immaculate condition, however, freshly painted pristine white, window frames and trim a light, minty green.

Things were a lot looser those days. When I didn't get a response to my knock, I went around back, knocked again there, then shimmed the kitchen door. If it ever came to it, I'd just say the door was ajar, I heard sounds inside, suspected intruders.

Three rooms. Kitchen with counters and stove immaculate, bath just off it to the right, living room straight ahead, bedroom to the left. That's where I found her. She was propped up with pillows, dressed in a pale pink nightgown with small blue flowers at neck and hem and larger blue flowers for buttons. Her hair, clean and bright, lay on the pillow, framing a face wherein eyes rolled left, right, left. Mucus ran out of one nostril and snailed towards the slack mouth.

"Please don't hurt her," a voice said behind me.

I told him I wouldn't, told him who I was.

"I've been out shopping. I never leave her alone any more than I have to." He put the bag of groceries on the floor by the door. "She needs changing. All right if I do that?"

Yes.

Going to the bed, he unbuttoned the nightgown and unpinned the towel doing service as diaper. The strong chemical smell of her feces spilled into the room. He took the diaper into the bathroom, to a covered pail there. He ran water till it was warm, and wet a facecloth. Brought it out and, holding her up effortlessly with the flat of one arm, wiped her clean. He took the facecloth back into the bathroom, rinsed and hung it on a rack there, washed his hands. He replaced the diaper, buttoned her gown and smoothed it. Then reached up to snap a fingernail against the IV feed, checking patency, drip rate, level.

"I thought I'd have longer with her. Just the two of us."

"I'm sorry."

He hadn't meant for this to happen, he told me, standing there looking down at her, into her face; hadn't intended to cause any trouble. He only wanted to take care of her. That's what he'd been doing at Parkview, for a long time now. Cleaning and bathing her, seeing after her feeds. But there was always too much else to do, too many others needing attention. She deserved better than that.

"What will happen to her now?"

"She'll go back to the hospital."

"Parkview, you mean."

"Right."

"And I'll be going to jail."

"For a while."

"Any notion how long?"

"Hard to say." God knows what they'd charge him with. Kidnapping, endangerment? Excessive kindness? "A year, eighteen months, something like that. After that you'd be on probation."

He nodded.

"Once I'm out, I'll be able to visit her."

# Chapter Nine

BREAKFAST WAS STRONG COFFEE and bagels. There were five kinds of bagels in a paper bag in the freezer (shipped in from Memphis? Little Rock?), butter, homemade fig preserves and cream cheese with chives below. Also a package of lox we both agreed should be put to rest. I washed my face and did what I could by way of brushing teeth while Val assembled it all; then, once we'd eaten, took care of the kitchen while she showered and dressed.

In the yellow Volvo on the way into town I thanked her.

She smiled. "Any time. It's a pleasure to have someone to talk to. You like my house?"

"I like your house a lot."

At the office she signed out the forensics kit and told us she'd be in touch when word came down. I walked her to the car.

"You get caught in town again, there's always my spare room," she said.

"I'll keep that in mind. Thanks."

"Take care of yourself, Turner."

I watched till the Volvo was out of sight. Eyes swiveled

towards me when I went back in the office.

"Guess you two hit it off," Don Lee said.

"Guess we did."

"House look good?" This from Sheriff Bates.

You'd better believe it, I said, and filled him in on what I'd seen. Floors taken down to bare wood, missing pieces of banisters and mouldings pieced in, layers of paint painstakingly rubbed away.

"Wish there were more like her," Bates said. "Most of those old places have been torn down by now. Or fallen down. We won't ever see their like again. Coffee?"

"Sure thing." I chewed my way through half a cup of it. Busy day in town. Every four or five minutes a car passed outside. The phone rang and went on ringing in the real estate office next door.

"The mayor's mail?"

"Beg pardon?" Don Lee.

"What you found on the body. Outgoing mail or incoming? Circulars? Bills? Bank statements? Personal letters?"

"Bills, mostly. That's what he put out for pickup. Clipped them to the front of his mailbox with a clothespin. Same clothespin's been out there eight or ten years."

"His mailbox at home."

"Right."

"On the porch or streetside?"

"These parts, they're all by the street."

As Bates was pouring more coffee, a fortyish woman pulled the door open and stepped in. She stopped just inside, blinking. Ankle-length pants that had started off black and with repeated washings gone purplish gray, red-and-blue flannel shirt over maroonish T-shirt. She was tall. The shirt's sleeves, left unbuttoned, came halfway up her forearms.

"Billie," Don Lee said. "How you doing?"

"C. R.'s left again."

"Honey, he'll be back. He always comes back. You know that."

"Not this time."

"Course he will."

"You think so?"

Bates walked over to her. For a moment before she looked off, their eyes met.

"Thought he liked the new job."

"Job was okay, Sheriff. What he didn't like was me."

Steering her to the desk, Bates said, "You had any breakfast? I could call across, have something sent over."

"Kids ate good this morning."

"They always do."

"Pancakes."

"Billie does great pancakes," Don Lee told me.

"Put pecans in, the way they like them." Her eyes swept the ceiling. "Woodie has to turn in his geography project today. I made sure he packed it up safe."

"You get any sleep, sweetheart?" Bates asked.

"I don't think so. I made brownies, for the kids. C. R. likes them too. It was dark outside. I think maybe I burned them."

"Don Lee, why don't you take Billie on home, see she gets settled in. That be okay with you, Billie?"

She looked wildly about for a moment at the door, window and floor, then nodded.

"He'll take her out by the ballpark," Bates said once they'd left. "They'll sit in the bleachers a while. Don't know why, but that always seems to calm her down."

"Is she okay?"

"Basically. You couldn't ask for a better person. Just sometimes, every six or eight weeks, things get too much for her. Get too much for all of us sometimes, don't they?"

I nodded.

"Been going on for three or four months, we figure—the missing mail. That's how far in arrears the mayor's bills had fallen. Gas, water, electric. Near as we can tell, he didn't know."

"Which tells us he doesn't bother balancing his checkbook."

"Mm-hm."

"And service was still being provided?"

"Things don't get shut off much 'round here. Just not the way we do it. And he's the mayor, after all."

"What about credit cards?"

"Looks like he paid those from the office. Those and the phone bill."

"He works at home?"

"Town this size, there's not a lot of mayoring needs doing. Not much call for regular office hours."

"So why would he pay the phone bill at the office? Some reason he doesn't want his wife seeing the bill, maybe? I assume there's a wife."

"Oh," Bates said, "there's a wife sure enough."

"Can we get a warrant for his phone bills? Home and at the office? See who he called, who called him?"

"No need for all that." He grabbed the phone and dialed, spoke a minute or two and hung up. "Faxing it over. Give her half an hour, Miss Jean says."

"That simple."

"Seems simple to you, does it?"

I understood. As a cop on city streets you learn to dodge, duck, go along, feint. You find out what works and you use it. Same here, just that different things worked.

"Where's the mayor live?"

"Out on Sycamore. Far end of town."

"Anyone else on that route have mail missing?"

"There's only the one route. And if so, they didn't notice."

"Or didn't report it."

Mug cradled in both hands, Bates swung his chair several degrees right, right knee rising to a point northeast, then a few degrees left, right knee dipping as the left V'ed northwest. "Hard as this may be for you to believe, Detective, we did get around to asking after that. Took us a few days to think of it, most likely. Probably have it written down somewhere."

"I don't mean any disrespect, Sheriff. I'm only here because you asked me, doing the job you asked me to do the only way I know how."

Our eyes met.

"All right," he said at length.

"So you found the mayor's mail in this guy's pocket."

"Right."

"But no wallet, no identification."

He shook his head.

"Don Lee mentioned a notebook."

"Nothing much there, far as we could tell."

"And he'd been holding some of this mail for what? Three, four months?"

"Right."

"Thought he was some kind of postman," I said. "Undelivering mail."

# Chapter Ten

I'D KNOWN SALLY GENE FOR two or three years. She'd done a couple of ride-alongs back when she started with Child and Family. I remember giving her a hard time, claiming she couldn't be much older than the children she was investigating, and her saying, "You're kidding me, right," my partner not getting it at all. Sally Gene and I had crossed paths professionally five, six times since. What she did was to her the most important thing in the world. I think deep down it may have been the only thing she really cared about. A lot of people who are outstanding at what they do seem to be like that. The rest of us look on, at once admiring and critical; vaguely ashamed of ourselves and our wayward lives.

That Sunday, she was waiting for me outside the station house.

"Think I might get a ride, Detective?"

"Sure thing, little girl."

She'd already cleared it with brass. Bill took one look at us coming out together, chucked me the keys, and got in back. "What the hell. So we give up an hour or two of knock-on-doors-and-ask-questions excitement."

Recently the department had bolstered the auto pool with half a dozen new blue Plymouths. We pretended we were being sly, but two guys that looked like Joe Friday driving around in a plain car with no chrome trim, black tires and no radio were pretty obvious.

"And what lovely suburb of the city might the three of us be touring today?" Bill said.

Round about the airport, as it turned out, in those years an undeveloped region of cheap motels and eateries. We nosed down the highway that led into Mississippi and turned off into a subdivison of tiny, plain houses once part of the army base. Trucks sold pecans, watermelons and peaches at the side of the road. The smell of figs and honeysuckle was everywhere.

I stood a few paces back as Sally Gene knocked. We weren't supposed to have much of a presence on these calls. Bill stayed by the car. I'd already had a look around. A vegetable patch ran alongside the west side beneath a double clothesline, okra, tomatoes and green peppers, all of it pretty much gone from lack of care. No car in the driveway, and what oil spills there were, were old ones. Four or five *Press-Scimitars* lay unrolled and unread at the back of the driveway, one near the front door, another halfway into the front yard.

The door opened. Flat, uninflected sound of TV from within. Cartoons, maybe, or a sitcom. But then I heard "Willa Cather tried in her own inimitable way ..." I watched Sally Gene's head tilt forward and down as the door came open. A child's face stared up at us. Twelve, maybe. Wearing a yellow nylon shirt he'd grow into in another four or five years and a serious expression.

"Daddy says not to let anyone in."

Sally Gene introduced herself.

"Daddy says not to let anyone in."

"I told you my name. What's yours?"

"William."

"William. I'm sorry, I know this is confusing, and I'm not saying your daddy was wrong, he wasn't. But I have to come in. Hey: I'd rather be home watching TV, too. But the people I work for tell me I have to come in and look around. They're kind of like your parents, you know? Always telling me what I have to do?"

The merest flicker as his eyes strayed to me, but I caught it. He was looking for a way out.

"How you doing, William?" I said. "Friends ever call you Bill?"

After a moment he shook his head.

"You hungry, William?"

Again the head went right, left, right. "I fixed breakfast. I know how to cook. I have a load of clothes in the dryer. Oughta get them out."

"Are your parents home, William?"

"They'll be back soon."

"How long have they been gone, William?"

He just looked at me. More than he could handle, I guess. Like so many things in his life.

"Miss Sally Gene and I need to come inside. Look: here's my badge. You hold on to it till I'm ready to leave. That should be okay, shouldn't it?"

After a moment he nodded and undid the chain.

In one bedroom we found a four-year-old girl locked in a closet. She'd very carefully defecated only in the rear corner by boots and old shoes, but urine had gone its own way, she'd had no control over that. A plate near the front held frankfurters and slices of American cheese.

In the bathroom a younger child with severe diarrhea, maybe two or three, was lashed by brown twine to the bathtub faucets. A Boy Scout manual on the back of the toilet bore a folded square of toilet paper at a section on knots. Jars of applesauce and peanut butter and plastic spoons sat within reach.

In a rear bedroom with bunk beds stacked north, south and east, children of various ages, six of them, sat straight-backed as army recruits. Their eyes swiveled to us as we came in. Plates of cold cuts and Oreo cookies sat on windowsills.

"I had no idea," Sally Gene told me.

"You must have."

"Oh, I knew something was wrong. But this …"

"Foster home?"

"One of the few we've never had complaints about. No trouble at all."

"I found a credit card in the desk drawer." William stood in the doorway behind us. "We haven't had real food for a long time."

"A Visa," Sally Gene told me, "and well past its limit. Two days ago someone tried to use its mate down in Vicksburg to settle a hotel bill that included an impressive bar tab. The card got confiscated."

"Foster parents?"

"Their card, anyway."

"I'm sorry," William said. "I know it was wrong."

"You did okay, son."

"You did great," Sally Gene said.

"Daddy put me in charge. I was just trying—"

"Who the fuck are you people?"

We both turned. He held a 12-gauge shotgun.

"Daddy!" The boy had moved on into the room beside us.

"And what are you doing in my house?"

I looked at Sally Gene, who fed me the name: "Sammy Lee Davis."

"Just stay cool, Mr. Davis, okay? I'm Detective Turner, Miss Lawson here's from city social services. We need to talk to you, that's all, just talk. Why don't you start by putting the gun down. There's a lot of kids in here, man. No one wants to see the kids get hurt. William: show your father my badge?"

The boy held it out.

"You're trespassing."

Thinking this wasn't the best time to discuss probable cause and his being at any time open to public inspection as a foster parent, I said, "Well, yes sir, truth is, we are. I can appreciate that's how it must look to you."

"You're the son of a bitch ran off with my wife, aren't you?"

The 12-gauge went to his shoulder. I have to give it to Sally Gene. She never once blinked, flinched or cut her eyes. He saw it in the boy's face, though, and turned just in time to take Bill's riot stick square on the forehead.

"You guys through with your business yet?" Bill said. "It's getting hot out there and I'm getting hungry. And that goddamn magnolia smells to high heaven."

# Chapter Eleven

SETH MCEVOY PLAYED QUARTERBACK, was a top band member, and had a four-point average. He also, judging from the photo on his computer desk, went with the prettiest girl in town. Kind of kid you hated when you were back in school, couldn't do anything wrong.

Don Lee came with me. We'd spoken with the boy's mother downstairs. Seth was busy filling out college applications. All the pictures on his walls hung perfectly straight. The spines of the books in the bookcase behind the door were all flush.

"How come you're so much older than the sheriff and Don Lee?"

"Mr. Turner's retired, Seth. He's agreed to help us out, more or less as a consultant."

You could see the intelligence in his eyes, the interest. He'd rather ask questions than answer them. He knew about his world. Knew it too well, perhaps. Now he wanted to know about other people's.

"So what can I do for you?"

"I was hoping you could tell me again what happened."

"I don't think there's anything I can add to what I told the sheriff." But he went along, forever the good kid, reciting all but verbatim what was in the official report. With time and retelling the story had baked to hard clay; nothing new or surprising was likely to peer out of doorways or corners.

"Sarah stopped because she saw something move."

"Said she did. You're gonna talk to her, too, though— right?"

I nodded. "She didn't scream, anything like that."

"Unh-unh. She just pushed herself up in the seat and said, 'Seth, what is that?' I didn't see anything, but I got out of the car and went to look. After a minute she came up behind me."

"Was there blood?"

"Not near as much as you'd expect. I remember thinking then how that made it all seem so much stranger. Just that hunk of wood sticking up out of him, and everything arranged so neatly there by him like he was, I don't know, in his room at home."

"Were there field mice around, rats, anything like that?"

"If there were, we didn't see them." He looked full at me. "Why would you ask that?"

"No real reason. What you do is, you go ahead and ask whatever comes to mind, never mind if it makes sense or not, just trying to get the shape of the thing, hoping it might shake something loose."

"For you, or for me?"

"I'd settle for either."

"Interesting." He jotted something down on a notepad beside him.

"How long have you and Sarah been dating?"

"Sarah and I aren't dating. We just hang out together."

"In the driveways of unoccupied houses."

He started to say more, then shrugged.

I glanced pointedly at the photograph on his desk. "What does *she* have to say about that?"

"A lot. Pretty much nonstop. But Sarah … Sarah and I have been friends a long time. A lot of the others don't like her, think she's weird. But there aren't many people around you can have a conversation with, talk about the things you think are important. Look, you're from the city, right?"

"Yeah. But the place I came from's a lot like this one."

He nodded. "Then maybe you know how it is."

★ ★ ★

I HAD NO IDEA WHAT WAS playing on her CD. I wouldn't even have known what to call it. It wasn't like any rock and roll I'd ever heard. And it wasn't on her CD player at all, as it turned out, but coming directly off her computer.

Music's the first handhold you lose in growing old, I thought as we made our way down narrow wood stairs to the basement Sarah Perkins had claimed as her own. The stairs were plain, untreated planks set into notches in doubled two-by-fours, heads of ten-penny nails dark against them. Sarah sat below in a pool of light. The music washed up from below, too, a drain in reverse. To me, it sounded like a slurry of things recorded from nature—cricket calls, footsteps over gravel, apples falling—then tweaked beyond recognition.

Sarah turned in her chair as we stepped onto the cement floor. Years ago, someone had laid in a frame of two-by-fours, started putting up Sheetrock, even tacked up one wall of cheap woodgrain paneling before abandoning the project. Sarah had covered the spaces with old album covers (mostly 1950s jazz), movie posters (a decided taste for horror films) and a hodgepodge of pieces of dark fabric of every conceivable size, shape and texture. Books were stacked against every wall. But mostly the room took its form from the U-shaped desk within which Sarah sat in the midst of three or four computers, and as many monitors, along with various cross-connected black boxes, scanners and the like. The huge half-dark, half-bright room was the inside of her head, this the cockpit from which she kept it on course.

Almost instantly, she broke into Don Lee's introduction. "How's Seth?"

"He's fine," I said. "You two haven't seen one another?"

"Our parents won't let us. Here." She handed across one of those clear folders with a plastic piece that slips over the edge to bind it. "This should help. *And* save time."

Don Lee looked at it a moment and handed it to me. The cover read, in small capitals: INCIDENT OF THE NIGHT OF MAY 14. Then, following a two-line space: AS AVERRED BY SARAH PERKINS. Below that, her address, phone number, two e-mail addresses and a signature.

Inside, with approximate times, was a step-by-step listing of her and Seth McEvoy's arrival at the subdivision, their pulling into the driveway, her first sight of what she believed to be movement, their investigation of same and subsequent call to the police. She had fixed the times by checking her memory of the music being played against the radio station's log.

"I have a good ear for music, and excellent recall," she said. Oh?

The second page of her report recounted what she and

Seth had said to one another, beginning with "Seth, what is that?" and ending only with them saying good-bye when her parents (her mother, actually) picked her up at the police station. The third and fourth pages held computer-generated diagrams of relative positions: car, body, moonlight, the man's belongings, the stake.

"Thank you," I said.

"You're welcome, Mr. Turner. Is there anything else?"

"Tell you the truth, I don't know. I'm kind of over-whelmed here." I had another look. "This is great." After a moment I said, "Seth told me you and he aren't dating."

"Seth and I are friends."

"Friends. That's one of those words that can mean different things to different people."

"Words are like that." She smiled at me. "Aren't they?"

"He also told me his girlfriend—what's her name, again?"

"Emily."

"That Emily isn't too happy about you and Seth spending so much time together."

"Imagine that." A couple of bells sounded somewhere in her instrument panel. She glanced briefly down. "Do you know what a truffle is, Mr. Turner?"

"More or less, I think."

"They're tubers. They grow underground, on the roots of trees that have spent years earning their place, struggling for it, working their way up into the light. The tuber lives off the tree and gives nothing back."

"Okay."

"Emily is a truffle."

★ ★ ★

"DOC OLDHAM TAKES CARE of most ever'thing medical 'round here."

"Even had a look at Danny Bartlett's cows last year when they came up frothing at the mouth," Don Lee said. "Been known to pull a tooth or two, need be."

"He had a few choice words to say about my bothering him, but he's on his way."

"I could have gone to see him."

"I offered. Said he had to come into goddamn town anyway, he just hadn't goddamn it planned on it being so goddamn early."

"Barks a lot, does he?"

The sheriff nodded as the door opened and, borne on a flood of badinage, Doc Oldham entered. "Goddamn it, Bates, what's the matter with you, you can't handle a simple thing like this without hollering for help. This here your city boy?"

*Boy*—though we were much of an age. I nodded, which seemed the safest way to go at the time.

The sheriff introduced us.

"Don't talk much, does he?"

"You looked like you had more to say. I figured I'd best just wait till you wound down."

"I don't wind down. I ain't wound down in sixty-some years now and I don't aim to start. What the hell, you got coffee here to offer a man or not?" Don Lee was already pouring one, and handed it over. "Worked up to Memphis, I'm told."

"Yes, sir."

"You like it?"

"The city, or the work?"

"Both."

"I liked the work. The city, I got to liking less and less."

"'Spect you did. Saw things from the other side for a spell too, I hear."

"Didn't much like that either."

"Make the city look right tame?"

"Most ways it *was* the city—just a smaller version. Same tedium, same hierarchies, same violence and rage."

"Goddamn it, Bates, I will say one thing for you. You send for help, at least you got the decent good sense to bring in someone able to find his own head in the dark."

The sheriff nodded.

"And he ain't talkin' all the time like some others. Momma brought him up right."

"Actually, sir, it was my sister. Our mother passed when I was five."

"How much older was your sister?"

"She was sixteen."

"Good woman?"

"The best. Lives out in Arizona now, has three kids."

"Bringing up her *second* family."

I nodded.

"My folks disappeared when I was fifteen," Doc said. "We never did find out what became of them. There were two kids younger than me, one older. I was the one took care of us. It's a miracle, but we all turned out all right."

"That's what families are all about."

"Used to be, anyhow." He finished his coffee, put the mug down on the desk, and slid it towards Don Lee, who went to refill it. "You wanna put some goddamn sugar in this one to kill the taste?" Doc said. Then to me: "What'd you need?"

"Considering what I have, just about anything would be welcome."

"You read the file?"

"Sheriff Bates showed it to me."

"Don't know as I can add much to what's there."

"You didn't do the autopsy yourself, right?"

"Just the preliminary. Autopsy gets done up to the capital. Technically speaking I'm just coroner. Hereabouts that's an elected position, doesn't even require medical training."

Don Lee began, "It's an important—"

"It's political bullshit's what it is. Nobody else would take it, and for damn good reason."

"The body had been there a while, you said."

"Been there alive for some time before he was there dead, and that was three, four days."

"The stake had been driven in there?"

"No way. Where he lay'd be my guess. Someone mopped up as best he could. Lot of blood trace still. The bedding was rolled. Makes me think maybe he'd come back, laid down to rest thinking he'd go back out."

"So the body got moved."

"Absolutely. Some point after the stake went in—dead or almost, really no way to tell—he got wired to that trellis."

"Blood and skin under his nails?"

"Looked to be. Could just be dirt, grease."

"Maybe that'll give us something. I assume State'll do blood typing, run the DNA?"

"Blood, yes. Anything heavier'n that gets shipped out to Little Rock or Memphis, one of the big labs."

"You're saying be patient."

"Be very patient."

"Nothing else?"

I looked around the room in turn. Bates shook his head, as did Don Lee.

"One thing I have been thinking on," Doc said.

"Okay."

"This man's been out there, on the street, a while."

"Three, four months at least. Probably a lot longer."

"So how's it come about he has soft hands?"

# Chapter Twelve

FOR YEARS IT WAS KNOWN AROUND THE department as the Monkey Ward caper.

We got tagged midday one Saturday. Dispatch was sending out a black-and-white, but the Lieutenant wanted detectives to rendezvous. Half a dozen calls had come in about whatever the hell was going on out there.

It was one of those new developments north of Poplar near East High School, reclaimed land where long-boarded-up storefronts, restaurants and thrift shops were being leveled to create inner-city suburbs, row upon row of sweet little perfect houses each with its own sweet front and rear lawn.

When we pulled up, one of the guys had a hedge trimmer, the other one a posthole digger. Took us some time to sort out they were in each other's yards. They'd gone from insults across the fence to a swinging match, and when that did neither of them much good, they'd opted for technical support. One was busily defoliating every bush and small tree on his neighbor's lawn, including plants in window boxes. The other was busily making the next yard look like a convention of moles had just let out.

The uniforms had just about talked them down by the time we got there. These guys had been riding together for fifteen, sixteen years; everyone in the department knew them. Tall one was Greaser, named for the hair tonic he must have bought in quart jars. Short one was Boots, for the zip-up imported footwear always polished to a high shine. Light reflected off Greaser's hair or Boots's boots could blind you.

Boots had Mr. Ditch Witch, Greaser had Hedge Man. They'd persuaded them to lay down the appliances and were bringing them together as we arrived. Close-up disputes like that, it's always a kind of square dance, swing them apart, bring them together, open it up again. As we climbed out of the car, the two had just shaken hands and were talking. Next thing we knew, they'd grabbed up a garden hoe and a leaf rake and were going after one another again, Robin and Little John with quarterstaffs on that narrow bridge. Should have been on riding mowers, galloping towards one another, lances at ready.

Randy looked across the top of the car shaking his head and said he knew all along it was gonna be one of those days. About that time the hoe caught Greaser hard on the side of the head. He'd moved in to intercede, baton high to protect himself, then half-turned to check on the other guy's position. Went down like a burnt match.

"You see that?" Randy said later. "Hair didn't move at all. What *is* that shit he puts on it?"

The citizen let the blade of the hoe fall to the ground, handle in his hand. Jesus, what had he done. But the one with the rake was still charging toward him, teeth aloft like a giant bird claw. Then his left foot stepped over a garden hose, we saw Boots run between them, suddenly Boots was behind the guy, still had hold of the hose, now he was pulling it tight—and the guy slammed to the ground.

Randy stood shaking his head. "Sure hope he don't aim to hog-tie him, too."

"I'll call it in," I said.

Doctors stitched it as best they could, but the hoe had opened it up even better, and Greaser wound up with a scar that ran an inch and a half or so down his forehead over the left eye. He took to pasting a lock of hair in place over it.

"Missiles take out civilization as we know it," Randy said, "that hair of his'll still be perfect."

# Chapter Thirteen

WEDNESDAY HAD GONE BY, THAT was the day Bates came and collected me and the night I stayed at Val's, then Thursday, when I'd interviewed the two kids and Doc Oldham. Now it was Friday. I'd slept on the office couch, awake at 10:35, 11:13, 2:09, 3:30, 5:18, 6:10. (Ah, the digital life. Never any doubt where you stand.) From time to time the radio crackled. The faucet in the bathroom had an on-again, off-again drip. Now someone was hammering boards in place over the windows.

No, someone's knocking at the door. And Don Lee is heading that way. Coffee burps and burbles in the maker, aroma spreading insidiously through the room like an oil spill. I'm fascinated by the fact that the door to the sheriff's office is locked. One of those weird things in life that seems to be the setup for a punch line you never quite get to.

A woman came in as I struggled up from the couch. She wore a tailored, narrow-waisted business suit the like of which don't seem to be around much anymore. The suit was green. So were her eyes. They went from Don Lee to me and back. Obviously she wondered if I shouldn't be in one of the cells, instead of out here.

"Sheriff Bates?"

Behind her soft urban lilt was a hill-country accent, East Virginia maybe. Getting along in years, and it hadn't stuck its head up to look around for a time, but it was still there. Don Lee said who he was and asked if he could help her.

"Sarah Hazelwood." She held out her hand to shake his, not something you saw a lot with women in this part of the country even now. "From St. Louis."

"Not originally, though," I put in, God knows why. I'd escaped the couch's hold by then. Her eyes met mine at a level. That was a harder hold.

"We're from where we choose to be. And what we choose to be."

Turning back to Don Lee, she went on.

"I'm looking for my brother. He ... dropped out, I suppose is the right word—disappeared—almost a year ago."

"From St. Louis."

"Fort Smith. He lives ... lived ... at home, with our father. And this isn't the first time he managed to go missing, by any means. But always, before, he'd turn up again in a week or two. We'd get a call from an ER in Clarksdale or West Memphis, or from the police down in Vicksburg, and go fetch him."

"And now you think he's here?" Me again.

Again, those eyes level with my own: "You are ... ?"

Don Lee introduced us, explaining my function as consultant. That word just kind of hung there in midair, letters malformed, dripping paint.

"We've reason to believe he may be."

Don Lee had poured his own and was adding in sugar

before it occurred to him. "Like some coffee, Miss Hazelwood?"

"No, but thank you."

"And your reason is?" I said. "For believing he's here, I mean."

"I work as a paralegal, for the firm of Scott and Waldrop. We handle estates, trust funds, endowments. That sort of thing."

"Good work if you can get it," I said, with little idea why I was baiting this woman.

"The firm has nine attorneys, Mr. Turner. Two by choice work full-time at immigration, wrongful termination, civil-rights issues. Mostly pro bono."

"I apologize. Sometimes I get up in the morning and find I've gone to bed with this absolute jerk."

"How does the jerk feel about it?" After a moment she added: "I accept your apology."

Don Lee cleared his throat. "You've come all the way from St. Louis?"

"I flew into Memphis yesterday afternoon. We drove up from Fort Smith this morning."

"We?"

A black woman wearing a full-length dress slit on both sides to the upper thigh stepped through the door and stood there blinking. Earth colors, print, vaguely African. "Sorry to interrupt, but Dad's not doing so well out here." Clipped short, her hair directed attention to the long, graceful curve of her neck, high cheekbones, shapely head. The dress was sleeveless, showing well-developed shoulders and biceps.

Moments later, the second woman—Adrienne, as I was soon to learn—pushed a wheelchair through the door Miss

Hazelwood held open. In it sat a man with what looked to be a military brush cut. Ever seen a porch whose supports on one side have been kicked out? That's what he reminded me of. Everything on the right side, from forehead down through mouth to foot, sagged. That much closer to the earth we all wind up in.

"Daddy, this is Deputy Sheriff Don Lee. And Mr. Turner. Memphis police, I think."

Adrienne rolled the chair into a corner away from the heat of morning light.

"This okay, Mr. H?"

He turned his head to nod and smile at her. The right side of his face gave the impression of trying to stay in place, moving half a beat behind, even as the left side turned. Same with the smile. Left side voted yes, right side abstained.

Adrienne and Sarah Hazelwood exchanged gazes filled with wordless information.

"In St. Louis," Miss Hazelwood said, "at Scott and Waldrop, we handle a lot of legal work for the county. Mostly it's clerical, routine. Getting papers filed on time, filling in forms. But we also represented Sheriff Lansdale in a wrongful-death suit last year when a sixteen-year-old died of asthma while being held in his jail."

"Black?" I glanced at Adrienne. No reaction.

Miss Hazelwood nodded. "We've maintained something of a special relationship since then. Dave Strong heads up Information Services. Created and pretty much runs the computer system and database single-handed. He's my contact there."

"You hitched a ride on the information superhighway," I said.

This time she almost smiled.

"Two days ago, according to parameters he'd set, his computer flagged a bulletin. An unidentified murder victim whose description matched my brother's. Dave pulled down prints, and they matched too."

"I sent the bulletin," Don Lee said. "We put prints out on the wire, too, but nothing came back."

"We have a set taken on one of Carl's admissions to a psychiatric hospital, expressly for the hospital's own use, never broadcast. Sheriff Lansdale's people compared them for us."

Later, in the back room of Dunne's Funeral Parlor, which doubled as morgue, standing beside her father with one hand lightly on his shoulder, Sarah Hazelwood said, "Yes. That's Carl," and looked—not quickly or nervously but cautiously—from Adrienne to her father. Everyone bearing up as well as could be expected. Better, actually, given the circumstances.

"So there's one of us poor bastards put to rest, at least," Doc Oldham said. He sipped coffee, then, frowning, sniffed the mug. It bore the photo of a man's face that, when hot liquid got poured in, by degrees became a skull. "Damn milk went south at least a day ago. I wanted buttermilk, I'd of ordered up cornbread to go with it."

"They said back home he'd sit out on the porch half the morning waiting for the mail to come."

"So you were right," Bates said. "About him thinking he was a postman. Wouldn't think he'd be likely to be getting much mail."

"But he *could* have. That's what it was all about. Anticipation, promise. Like the world's holding its breath, and for just that one moment anything can happen, anything's possible."

"Doesn't sound like his life was exactly awash with possible."

"Okay, okay. Business you had here is over," Doc Oldham suddenly announced. "Anybody alive, able to move, you're out of here—now. Dead folk and me've got work to do."

# Chapter Fourteen

RANDY WAS THE FUNNIEST MAN I ever knew. Back there at first, all those "hair'll last long as roaches and cigarette butts" remarks, I tried to keep up with him, even managed to do so for a while, but it flat wore me out. Before Randy came along, I'd had a clutch of temporary partners, among them Gardner, who died in a cheap motel listening to a prostitute's sad tale, and Bill, who I think may have said thirty words to me the whole time, twenty of those the day he cold-cocked Sammy Lee Davis when we found all those kids left alone; then I'd worked by myself again for a while. Randy was supposed to be temporary, too. Maybe the desk jockeys forgot where they put him, or maybe after Randy and I'd been together a few weeks they just up and decided what the hell, it ain't broke…

Boy was Jewish, God help him, problematic those days outside the shelter of owning, say, a jewelry or furniture store, but not even God proved much help to other cops who decided to make it an issue. They'd find themselves with new nicknames they couldn't shake off, enough jokes at their expense to bury them alive.

From the first, though, for reasons I never understood and still don't, I was somehow exempt.

"Pawnshop's right around this corner," I told him the first night we rolled out together. Following up on a double murder, possibly a murder-suicide, we had a long night of knocking-on-doors-and-asking-questions to look forward to. Car had the rearview mirror duct-taped to the side, and the seat jumped track whenever I hit the brakes. He made no secret of his heritage. Nor was I what you'd call a beacon of charity those days—and already he was wearing me down. "Want I should drop you?"

After a moment he said in perfect black dialect, "Nawsir. I be trying to 'similate."

Fact is, we got along great. The standing joke between us got to be if we didn't know better we might have thought the Captains knew what they were up to when they put us together. Guaranteed a laugh anywhere cops were.

And cops were most everywhere we went. Dinner at Nick's before going in on second watch, D-D's Diner noontime days, breakfast at Sambo's coming off long late nights, bars in the Overton Square area Randy and I went to afterwards to wind down. After a while it started getting to me. We don't see anyone *but* cops anymore, I told him one night.

"They're our family."

"You *have* a family."

His expression, in the moment before he checked its green card and deported it, told me more than I wanted to know. How much of recent behavior did that expression explain?

We'd have got into it then but got tagged. No patrols available, could we take it? Speak to the lady at 341 E.

Oakside, she'd be standing by the weeping willow out front. And she was, demanding to know before Randy and I even had the squad doors open what could be done about her son, could we please help her, no one should have to put up with this, she couldn't stand it any longer. The tree was huge, a wild green bouffant mimicking her blondish one, clay irrigation ports at its base. Near as I could tell, she didn't have those.

Her son, she told us, kept breaking into her house. Twenty-six years old and he wouldn't work, wouldn't do much of anything but hold down the couch, watch TV and eat. Whenever she brought it up he'd say he was going to do better, he knew all that, he was sorry, she had every right and so on, and she'd put up with it a while, but then he'd never follow through, so she'd toss him out again. Change locks, the whole works. But he'd just break in, be there on the couch like nothing happened when she got home. She'd had enough. She'd had it this time. She wanted his fat useless butt off her couch and out of her apartment and she wanted him to know that's how it was going to be from now on.

She couldn't get away right now, everybody else was out of the office, showing houses. Must she go along? Could we … ? Old Miss Santesson from across the alley had called to let her know that, after she left for work, Bobbie had gone over the back fence, kicked out the bathroom window and climbed through.

Some miles of heavy traffic to go. Randy called it in as we pulled away from the willow's shade. Still holding the mike, he looked out his window and said, "Things haven't been going real well between Dorey and me."

"So I figured."

He looked over at me.

"Kinda lost that sartorial edge you used to have," I said. "I'd of sworn I actually saw a spot on your coat one time last week."

"A spot."

"Try club soda."

"Club soda, right." He leaned forward to cradle the mike. "Couple starts having trouble, everyone says they're not spending enough time together. But it seems like the more we're together, the worse it gets."

"I'm sorry, man."

"Me too. So is Dorey. So are our folks. Everyone's sorry. Betty most of all." His daughter, what, fourteen now? "She doesn't say anything, pretends she doesn't know. But it's there in her eyes."

"Has to be hard."

"Scary thing's how easy it is, some ways."

Bobbie put up no struggle. He met us at the front door when we rang (one of the chimes then popular) and told us he knew, he knew, but she had no right, it was his house too. He went on saying that all the way downtown, eyes making contact in the rearview mirror above a stained orange sweatshirt. He was still saying it when we dropped him off at John Gaston ER on his way to the psych ward. By that time it was nearing shift's end and the station house loomed before us, this sudden cliff of bright lights, as we pulled up in our little hiccoughing skiff with side mirror flapping like a tiny, useless wing. Randy told me he'd do the paperwork.

"No way in hell."

"Hey—"

"Go home, Randy. Go home and hug your daughter, fix breakfast for your wife. Talk to them."

He didn't, of course. But at the time I wanted to think he might.

He called in the next day and again the one following. Captain pulled me over the third morning to see if I'd say anything about what was going on. He didn't ask outright or push, just told me he hoped Randy'd be back on his feet soon, that he'd never missed a single day before.

That night, I called.

Hey. Turner. Good to hear your voice, Randy said. Just I'm spending some time at home, he told me. Taking your advice. Taking it easy.

"You doing okay, then?"

"Better than that. Home-cooked meals every night. Meat loaf, mashed potatoes, gravy. Have the leftovers with biscuits next morning. Sorry to cut out on you like this, though. How's the bad guys?"

"Still winning. Don't stay out too long or we'll never catch up."

"I won't, then. See you soon, partner."

Two days later I went over there. It was twilight, color draining visibly from the world, leaves blurring on trees, shadows stepping in everywhere. Through a window set high in the front door I could see over the back of the couch to a coffee table piled with plates, glasses, hamburger wrappers and potato-chip bags. The TV was on, some local talent show for kids, picture rolling like clockwork every three seconds.

I rang the bell twice more, then opened the screen and banged on the door. Maybe try around back? Check with neighbors? I looked to the right, where a window curtain in the house next door fell closed, and looked back just as Randy's face came up over the couch. Kilroy. Just this half a face and the fingers of two hands. When I waved, one of the hands lifted to answer. Randy glanced at it in surprise. I expected him to get up and come around the couch, but instead he clambered over the back and, hitting the floor, did a little off-balance shuffle and recovery, Dick Van Dyke on a bad day. Closer to the door he stumbled for real.

"Hey," he said, "you want some coffee?" and without waiting for a reply went off opening drawers and closet doors and looking under chairs. "Got some here somewhere."

I went out to the kitchen. Sure enough, there it was. In a Corningware pot with blue flowers on it. The pot was full, and it had been sitting there for some time. But Randy wasn't drunk, as I first thought. It was worse.

When I walked by him, he'd followed me like a lost kitten. Now he went eye-to-eye with the little red light atop the handle.

*"There* it is!"

Took me over an hour to start getting any sense out of him. I poured Randy's vintage coffee down the drain, made more, and we sat at the kitchen table knocking it back. He was like a child. Like a boat cut loose, drifting wherever wind and current took it. I don't think he had any idea whether it was day or night, how long he'd been here like this, even that something might be wrong. Alone in the house with the world shut out, without landmark, limit or margin, he had drifted free.

Momentarily, intermittently, Randy came into focus and was able to tell me what happened.

Dorey had moved out a month ago. We'd been on second-shift rotation then, and he'd come home just after midnight to find the house dark, a single lamp burning in the living room on the long table inside the door where they always dropped mail. At the table's far end was a stack of freshly ironed shirts. Beside that, Dorey had laid out bills in the order they would come due, with postdated checks attached. Her note was leaning against the lamp.

*I love you but I won't be back. I'll send*
*an address when I have one. You'll be*
*welcome to see Betty any time, of course.*
*Please take care of yourself.*

It was signed, rather formally, "Doreen." Randy took the note out of his shirt pocket and handed it to me. It was broken-backed at the creases from much folding and unfolding. There were stains.

"I did all right at first," he said. "I'd come home, eat something, have a beer, and be okay. Start thinking: I'm gonna get through this."

"You should have told me."

"Yeah, well … Lots of things I should have done."

We talked a while longer, much of our dialogue making little sense, some of it making none, connectives torn away, grammarless sentences left dangling for the listener to punctuate or parse as he would. Eventually I left Randy at the kitchen table and went out to the phone in the hall. He was still in there talking to me.

I didn't bother calling Sally Gene at home, but after a number of tries tagged her at the Baptist psych unit. When a nurse handed the phone over, Sally Gene took it and said "I'm busy."

"You always are. I'm looking for my favorite social worker."

"Turner?"

"Your favorite driver. But this time, I'm the one who needs a ride-along."

I told her about Randy.

"Is he oriented?" Sally Gene asked.

"Comes and goes. Rest of the time, it's hard to tell."

"He knows you?"

"Yes."

"And once you started talking to him, he was able to lay out a sequence of events?"

"More or less."

"Has he been eating?"

Yes again. I'd looked in the refrigerator and found stacks of TV dinners.

"Alcohol?"

"Not that I know. I'd be surprised. Never much of a drinker, two or three beers'd be his limit. And I think he only did that to fit in."

"So what are we looking for here?"

"I don't know. We're on your ship, with this. You're the skipper."

"Little outside what I'm used to, what I do day to day. And it's been a while since I trained. We want to get him some help, obviously. Observation, at the very least… Any sign he's a danger to himself?"

"Not that I can see."

"We don't want to jam him up on the job, so we'll be wanting to keep it off the public record."

"If that's possible, great. But the most important thing's to help him dig out of this, whatever it takes."

"Okay, listen. Let me make a few calls. I'll get back to you.

What's the number there?"

I gave it to her and went out to the kitchen, where Randy, quiet at last, had fallen asleep with his head on the table. On the refrigerator, magnets shaped and painted as miniature vegetables held up sheaves of coupons and grocery receipts. A drawing his daughter Betty had done years ago hung under another magnet that first looked to be an angel or cherub but on closer inspection turned out to be a pig with wings.

"Hey, you're here!" Randy said.

Within the hour, we were checking him in at Southside Clinic. Set up to care for the indigent, Sally Gene told me when she called back, by a young doctor from up east, an idealistic sort, but damned good from all she heard. She'd made inquiries of colleagues, pretending she needed the information for one of her clients. Southside was expecting us. She'd meet us there.

# Chapter Fifteen

"THE THING WE CAN'T UNDERSTAND is who could possibly want to kill Carl. He was harmless, sweet. It would be like crushing a kitten. Nor do we have any idea what he was doing here, or how he got here in the first place, or why."

Sarah Hazelwood and I were sitting on the bench outside Manny's Dollar tore. Adrienne and Mr. Hazelwood had driven off to find rooms. I'd directed them to Ko-Z Kabins out by the highway. A longish drive, and the sort of place you apologize ahead of time for recommending, but what else was there.

"I take it you're all a family."

"Just like choosing where to be from, Mr. Turner. Families can be chosen too." She smiled. "I don't mean to be confrontational."

"I understand."

"Dad's not Adrienne's father, but she never treats him as if he's anything else. In some ways, she's closer to him than I am."

"You and Adrienne—"

"Half sisters. Mother had her before she married Dad,

when she wasn't much more than a girl herself. Adrienne was raised by grandparents. Then, not long after Mother died, Adrienne came looking for her. This wasn't supposed to be possible, with all kinds of blinds set up, but Hazelwoods are a resourceful lot. Adrienne and Dad got along famously from the first. She stayed with us for a few days, days became a week, eventually we all understood she wasn't going to leave. The rest developed slowly."

Whether to assess my reaction or judge if I needed further explanation of "the rest," Sarah Hazelwood regarded me steadily.

A huge grasshopper came out of nowhere and landed in the middle of the street. It sat there a moment then leapt on, heading out of town, glider-wings thrumming. Thing looked to be the size of a frog.

"Where does Carl fit in?"

"Mother was along in years when she had me. Her health was never good after. As I said before, where we belong, our families, we're able to choose those. Mother always said they pulled me out and pulled her plumbing right after."

A mockingbird swooped down at the grasshopper from behind, realized it didn't have time to clear Ben McAllister's truck coming towards them, bed crisscrossed with feed sacks, and flew back up. I waved at Ben, who nodded his usual quarter-inch. The grasshopper emerged from underneath and hopped on.

"One day Dad was out hunting. He happened to pass close by the neighbor's house a mile or so up the hill and heard a baby crying. He knocked, got no answer, and went on in. The house wasn't much more than a shack. A man named Amos Wright had been living there for as long as anyone could remember. Then a year or so back he'd suddenly turned up with a wife. No one knew where she came from, or how the two of them ever met. Amos had always kept to himself.

"Dad said he could smell the stench before he set foot on the porch. And when he went in there, the place was full of flies. They were buzzing all around the baby laying in its crib. The baby's mother was on the floor by the bed. Flies had laid eggs in her wounds and maggots were boiling up out of them."

"The baby—"

"The baby was Carl. Amos didn't have family that anyone knew of, and no one knew anything at all about the mother, so my folks took the boy in and raised him, the way country people will. Amos wasn't ever seen again, and they never did find out anything more about what happened. Some said it was an accident, others claimed someone must have broken in and beat the woman to death, maybe even a relative. A lot of people assumed Amos just up and killed her, of course, then ran."

"Carl knew about this?"

"Most of it. It was never easy to be sure how much or what Carl understood. Sometimes you'd be sitting there talking to him and you could all but see what you were telling him get … bent. You'd watch it start turning to something else inside him."

"Troubles came early, then."

"He seemed all right at first, Dad said. And for a while they shrugged it off. Hill folk have a high tolerance for peculiarities. Later, doctors told them it could have been from those days he was alone there in the cabin without food or water, no one knew for how long."

"Brain damage."

She nodded. "Possibly. But he'd had no prenatal care—or postnatal, for that matter. He'd been born right there in the cabin to all appearances. Easily could have suffered insult during birth, deprived of oxygen, too much pressure on the head, causing a bleed. Or he could have picked up an infection, either then or later on, passed on from his mother, carried by insects. Simple heredity? The mother never looked healthy or quite right herself, most said. For all that, my folks brought Carl up the same as me. They tried to, anyway. Not much about it was easy for them."

"Or for you, would be my guess."

"I liked having a brother. And it's not as though he was ever violent, anything like that. He just wasn't always *there*. I did have a few fights back when he started school. You know, taking up for him. But pretty soon the others left us alone."

"He finished school?"

"And got a job, working at Nelson Ranch. We'd moved by then, to the closest town. Called it a ranch, but what they raised was chickens."

"Takes a small lariat."

She looked at me oddly a moment, then laughed.

"Carl had been getting worse the past year or so. His mind would wander off and he'd go looking for it, Dad said. He got fired after a month or so. Mrs. Nelson came over herself to talk to Dad and tell him how bad they all felt. After that, he just hung around the house, I guess. I was off at college. At first I wrote to him, but he never answered, and we soon lost touch. We never had much of anything to say to one another the few times I came home."

"You didn't get home regularly?"

"I was paying my own way. I had a half-scholarship, but that didn't go near far enough. Every weekend, most breaks and holidays, most days after class, I was working."

"Good grades?"

"Good enough that I got my degree in three and a half years. I wanted to go on to law school, but there was no way I could afford it. The cupboards were bare."

"You're still young. You could go back."

She shook her head. "It's a question of confidence—confidence and momentum. Back then it never occurred to me that anything could stop me. I know too many things that can stop me now."

For reasons known only to himself (turndown on a date? bad test grade? failure to make the football squad?) a teenager leaning from a passing car shouted "I'm soooo disappointed."

Sarah Hazelwood smiled. "Well. There it is. What more need be said? For any of us."

# Chapter Sixteen

DOORS SLAMMING SHUT AND LOCKS falling: you never forget that sound, the way it makes you feel. That was something waiting in my own future, something I'd get used to, inasmuch as one ever does. Looking back even now, a familiar horror clutches at my throat, squeezes my heart in its fist.

When the buzzer sounded, I pushed through double doors into Wonderland. Here's another hall, another birth passage. Up two levels in an elevator crowded with bodies, down a cluttered hall—linen carts, food carriers, house-cleaning trucks—to the tollbooth. Nurses in a patchwork of whites, scrubs, Ban-Lon and T-shirts, jeans, slacks. One of them showed me into a double room where Randy, dressed in a jogging suit I'd packed for him, sat on one of the beds. Everything in the room, bedspread, curtains, towel folded neatly on the bedside table, was pastel. Randy's jogging suit was sky blue.

He looked up at me. "Stupid, huh?"

I had no idea how much he remembered, and asked him.

"All of it. But it's like a TV show I saw, or a movie. Like it's not me, I'm standing off somewhere watching: who *is* this asshole? Beats all, doesn't it?"

"I spoke with the Captain this morning. He's the only one back at the station house who knows what's going on. Wants me to tell you don't worry, he's got you covered."

Neither of us said anything else for a time.

"I appreciate this, buddy," Randy said finally.

"Hey. Don't get me wrong, you're no prize. But with you gone, either I head out alone or wind up having to take care of some half-assed retard no one else'll have. At least I'm used to you."

We both let the silence have its way again. After a while he said: "She's gone, isn't she?"

"Looks like it."

"I don't know what I'm going to do."

"Besides get your shit together and get back on the job, you mean."

"Yeah ... besides that."

A nurse came in with a tray. He held out his hand. She upended a fez-shaped container of pills onto it, handed him a small waxed cup of water. He drank and swallowed. She went away.

Anything I can get for you? I said. Anything I need to take care of?

He shook his head.

"Bills are all paid up. Plenty of food in the house... Unless you want to try to get in touch with Dorey, find out where she is."

I'd already done that, but I wasn't going to tell him. I said I'd look into it.

"I can't, I just can't," Dorey had told me. She was staying

with a friend on Clark Place, in an old red-brick house behind a screen of fig trees. We sat in wicker chairs on the enclosed front porch, behind a checkerboard of glass, struts and putty. Full of imperfections, each pane warped the world in a different way, reducing, enlarging, folding edges into centers, bending right angles to curves. Mockingbirds thrashed and sang in the fig trees. "Will you let me know how he is?" Dorey asked. I said I would.

"Gotta get back on the horse," I told Randy. "Anything you need, you'll call me, right?"

He promised he would.

"I'm so sorry," Marsha said that night over Mexican food. We'd been together six or eight weeks. A band looking like something from *The Cisco Kid* or a Roy Rogers movie, guitar, *bajo sexto* and trumpet, emerged from the kitchen playing "Happy Birthday" and stepped up to a table nearby. Our enchilada plates emerged moments later, pedestrian by comparison.

Marsha was a librarian. We'd met when a drunk fell asleep at one of the reading tables, she'd been unable to wake him at closing time, and, being right around the corner, I took the call. She was strikingly attractive, all the more so for never giving her appearance a thought one way or the other. Her mind was agile, the angle it might take at any given time unpredictable; good conversation sprang up spontaneously whenever she was around. Ten minutes after meeting someone, she'd be winnowing her way to the very best that person had. Despite my protests that it was important work I was good at, she kept insisting I was wasting my time as a detective.

"You remind me of my sister," I told her when she first

brought it up. "Always going on about how when I was young I'd been a natural leader, and she wondered why that changed."

"Did it?"

I shoveled about half a cup of salsa onto a chip and threw it back, washed it down with a long sip of Miller's.

"What happened, I think, was we grew apart."

"You and your sister?"

"Me and the other kids. We had everything in common at first. They weren't a particularly vocal or imaginative lot, and I'd just step up there, speak for them, pull them together. But as time went on, as we became individuals, our interests diverged. They took to sports, which I couldn't care about. I just never got it, you know? Still don't. Then I gravitated to books—every bit as mysterious to them, or more so."

Marsha reached over and got my beer, took a swig. Things liberated always taste better. "Just listen to yourself," she said. "Exactly what I mean."

Flagging down the waitress, I ordered another beer.

"Don't suppose you want one?" I asked Marsha.

"Me? A beer? Why on earth would I?"

"Just as I thought."

She forged ahead into enchiladas, refried beans and soggy pimiento-shot rice, bolstering same with occasional forksful from my plate, though it was identical with hers. Neither of us did well, finally, by the challenge. Fully half the food remained heaped on our plates when we were done, foil-wrapped tortillas untouched. I had another beer. We declined offers of take-home containers.

Out, then, into a typically fine southern evening, cicadae singing, moths beating at screens, quarter-moon above. My car waited. Beneath artificial lights its shiny, hard, blue-green body resembled nothing so much as the carapace of another insect.

"Randy doesn't have much to look forward to, does he?"

"Not right now."

"Without you, he'd have far less." She laid her head back against the seat. "It's so beautiful, you almost forget."

Years later in similar circumstances, in what might have been the same night inhabited by the great-great-grandchildren of those same cicadae, Val Bjorn turned her head to me and said, "A real Hank Williams night." As she hummed softly, the words came to me. A night so long ... Time goes slowly by ... His heart's as lonesome as mine.

# Chapter Seventeen

MUCH PRISON CONVERSATION consists of homilies, catchphrases, familiar incantations passed back and forth without thought. Someone gave voice to one of them, others within hearing would nod, that was an entire conversation. A particular favorite was: You don't use your time, it'll sure use you.

From every indication Carl Hazelwood had been well used by time, long before he wound up pinned like a specimen moth to a carport wall.

I'd barely got back to the office from talking to Sarah, who'd been picked up by Adrienne after she put their exhausted father to bed, when Don Lee answered the phone and handed it over.

Val Bjorn jumped right in. "Hey, I have your man. Had to hold my head right, figure out which way to look. His fingerprints ..." She trailed off. Because I'd not responded? "You had it already, didn't you?"

"Just."

"Day late and a dollar short."

I filled her in on the Hazelwood family's arrival. "Not that this in any way lessens my appreciation of your efforts, you know."

"You have no idea how hard I humped to get this."

"Maybe I can make it up to you."

"How *are* they? The family. They have any idea what might have gone down?"

"Mostly they're still trying to figure out what he was doing here."

"Aren't we all." She paused to sip at something. "What'd you have in mind with that making-up thing?"

"Dinner, maybe? I'm open to suggestion."

"You cook?"

"I buy."

"That could be a problem 'round here."

"So could my cooking."

"Hmmm. Then maybe I should cook. Lesser of two evils. Not a lot lesser, I'll admit."

"Or we could throw that whole food business over-board—"

"Quick footwork there, Turner. Look out below!"

"—and just have a drink."

"Done."

"There has to be a bar somewhere around here. I'll ask."

"Don't bother. I know just the place."

"Have a date, do we?" Don Lee said when I hung up.

We spent the day updating files on the murder, sorting medical reports and bits of information that had come in by e-mail and fax, reading back through it all, sifting, sorting, making lists. Like much of life, a murder investigation consists mainly of plodding along, circling back and waiting, considerably more low cleric than high adventure. Don Lee brought the sheriff up to speed on our visitors. Bates had called in a couple of times, around noon and again at three or so when we'd gone down to the diner for coffee, to see how we were doing, then showed up to take over not long after, just before daughter June went off duty at the desk. Father and daughter hugged, Bates and Don Lee did a quick shift report, most of it already covered by phone, and Don Lee headed home. I stayed around a while to talk things over. Then the sheriff dropped me off for my rendezvous with Val.

Just the Place turned out to be not a description but a proper name. Surrounded by a gravel parking lot, it sat in a clearing on a blacktop road three or four miles out of town. Just the Place was what folks back home called a beer joint, and most of them would have tipped over stone dead rather than get caught near one. Beer joints were for drunks—dagos and winos, people in blue jeans or greasy work clothes who drank up paychecks, beat wives, let kids go hungry and wild.

The inside looked pretty much what the outside, and old prejudices, promised. Val was sitting at the bar with a beer at half mast.

"I was gonna be a lady and wait—"

"Must have been a struggle."

"—but then I figured, what the hell."

"Objection sustained."

She raised her bottle in agreement. Moments later I managed to extract one of my own from the bartender, a woman with a western shirt straining at the snaps and big hair of the kind one rarely sees outside Texas. I expanded on what I'd already passed along about Carl and the rest of the Hazelwood clan. Their identification of the body, what they'd told me of his background, what I'd learned about them. Val said we'd be getting initial results on the forensics kit first thing in the morning by fax once the medical officer had had a look and signed off on it. Don't think it's gonna help much, though. Got some blood types and so on for you, but it's all generic.

Then she was telling me about a current case. She'd been in court from nine that morning till just before we met.

"Mostly I do family law. Almost a year ago, my client's husband got upset because she'd gone out to dinner with an old friend from high school. He went into their daughter's room, she was four at the time, and began beating her. The mother came home and found her there in the crib, eyes filmed over, slicks of mucus and blood on sheets printed with blue angels and pink rocking horses. The husband said he didn't know anything about it, the kid was fine the last time he looked in. My client moved out immediately, of course. But the girl had sustained significant brain damage. She's never recovered, she'll never develop mentally, even as her body continues to grow. Medical bills and maintenance costs are staggering. The husband's not paid a cent of child support."

"So you're going after him."

"Hardly. I represent the mother, but we're the defense. He's petitioning for full custody."

What could I say to that?

"No way he wants the child. Susie's a symbol, a possession. Like a couch or a painting, the contents of a lockbox."

"He has to hurt his wife once and for all, worse than ever before."

Val nodded.

I became aware that for some time there'd been activity

107

behind us, against the far wall. Now someone blew into a microphone and music started up. A simple riff on guitar, then a steel swelling behind, a long bass glide, drums. I turned on my bar stool, as did Val. We glanced at one another and moved to a table ringside.

"These guys are amazing," she said. "Just wait."

Interestingly, the band's front man and singer was black— the first black face I remembered seeing since moving back here. Save Adrienne's, of course, but she was an import. After a couple of Hank Williams songs and a creditable cover of "San Antonio Rose," the band locked onto Sonny Boy Williamson's "Gone So Long," taking it down home the same way early Texas string and swing bands had liberated "Sittin' on Top of the World" or "Milk Cow Blues," making it their own.

Fine stuff, followed by more. All of it purest amalgam country, voice calling, guitar responding, steel and bass laying a foundation, cellar, stairs. Chunks of Appalachian ballads, Delta blues, early jazz and Hawaiian floating about in there like vegetables in a rich stew.

"I once fell in love with a man because he had nothing but George Jones tapes in his apartment," Val said during an intermission.

"Is this something I need to know?"

"Think about it. It's a better reason than most others. I figured any man that devoted to Jones had to have something to him. Your lover's going to lose jobs, hair and interest in you, get fat, sit on the couch farting. Those tapes will still be there, still be the same, old George pouring his heart into every note. Always sounds like he's wrestling himself, squeezing notes out past some kind of emotional or physical obstruction. His voice stumbles, crawls and soars, always somehow at the very edge of what a voice is, what a man can feel." Dregs of a fourth beer went down her throat. She waved off another. "Sorry. I take this music seriously. Not many people do anymore. For a long time it was all that remained of our folk music. Now it's gone, or almost. Become just another part of the commercial blur."

By this time Eldon Brown, the band's singer, who, as it turned out, Val knew, had joined us. He sat with thin legs crossed, sipping from a cup the size of a goldfish bowl. Tea with honey and lemon, he said. For all his verisimilitudinous vocal renditions, not a trace of South or hill country in his speaking voice. Hoboken, New Jersey, he said when I asked.

"Family moved north during the war, looking for work. I grew up on local soul and gospel radio and this monster country station over in Carlyle, Pennsylvania. Came back south on tour with an R&B band, as guitarist, nine years ago, one of those last-minute pickup things. Third, fourth week into it, we're playing a bar in Clarksdale and the bass player takes after the singer with an oyster knife, to this day I don't know why. Not much left of the band at that point, but I stayed on. Been working steady ever since. Speaking of which ..."

He excused himself to take his place on the bandstand, kicking off with a no-holds-barred "Lovesick Blues," yodels slapping at the room's walls like a tide.

Val and I left around nine, picking our way out through packed bodies and a full parking lot. At her place we pulled cold cuts, cheese, pickles, olives and apples from the refrigerator and took them, with beers, out onto the front porch. It was a gorgeous, clear night, stars like spots of ice.

Wind worked fingers in the trees. An owl crossed the moon.

"It's good to have someone to talk to," Val said. She popped a bite of bologna into her mouth. The half-pound in her refrigerator (folks around here would call it an icebox) had come off the store's solid stick; we'd hacked it into cubes. "I'm not looking for anything more. I hope you know that."

Nor was I.

"You miss it?" she said.

"Someone to talk to—or something more?"

"Both, I guess." Her eyes met mine. "Either."

"Strange thing is, I don't. Not really."

Neither of us spoke for a time.

"I had a partner, back when I was a cop. His wife left him, took the kid, his whole life fell apart. One day I said to him it had to be hard. He looked across at me there in the squad car. Scary thing's how easy it is, he said."

After a moment she said, "I understand," and we sat silently in the wash of that amazing night, two people together alone under stars and pecan trees, personal histories tucked tight against our hearts as though to still or quieten them.

# Chapter Eighteen

YOU DON'T USE YOUR TIME, IT'LL sure use you. Don't talk it,
walk it. Putting money in the hat for those about to bail.
Passing around meager, prized possessions—sheets, T-shirts, a
transistor radio with extra batteries, Bob's Bodyshop
calendar—as you leave. Homilies, slogans, customs. A world of
things, objects. As though the narrowness and inaction of our
days had excised verbs themselves from our lives. (And the
pervasive violence an effort to reinvest them?) Everything
ended a few yards past our eyes; it had to. That's what you did
to get by, you drew everything in close to yourself, let short
sight take over. Soon enough, imagination, too, started
shutting down.

Homilies—and a lot of time staring at the join of cinder
blocks. Counting them, tracking where at one end of the
cell there's maybe a half-inch before the top line of mortar,
at the other end almost two. Or where a previous tenant
scraped away the mortar between blocks on the wall beside
his bed and the toilet. Did he spend that much time on the
toilet? Boredom, like blind faith, engenders strange errand
lists.

Nine hundred and sixty-four cinder blocks, from where I sat.

Six weeks in, I wrote away to New Orleans and Chicago for transcripts. Nothing about this endeavor proved easy. While you were allowed two letters a month postage provided, sending money remained a tricky prospect, and both schools required five-dollar fees. The prison chaplain came to my aid. Reading those transcripts once I got them was like looking in the mirror and finding someone else's face. Could I ever have been that callow? Had I actually taken a course called Revolutionary Precepts, and what on earth might it have been about? Two semesters of medieval history? I hadn't a single concept, movement or date left over from that.

Who *was* this person?

Someone, apparently, who'd been on the express train, a dozen or so stops away from getting a master's degree. Strange how I'd managed to forget that. Stranger still to wonder where all of it—all those hours and years of burrowing, the knowledge issuing from them, the ambition that led to them—might have gone. None of it seemed to be in me anymore.

By this time I'd suffered through a cellmate in the bunk above murmuring words aloud as he read from his Bible and another given to Donald Goines's *Whoreson, Swamp Man* and Kenyatta novels. Then Adrian came along, by which time I myself sat nose sunk like a tomahawk in college catalogs and bulletins. Our gray, featureless submarine went on plowing its way through gray, featureless days. And I, it seemed, while still submerged could complete my degree courtesy of the state that held me in such cautious esteem.

Nowadays, of course, in the house Internet Jack built, there'd be nothing much to it. But back then the labors involved proved Herculean. Each month or so I'd receive a thick envelope of material. I was expected to read through it, write the papers required and complete a test at its end, then mail the whole thing back, whereupon another envelope would arrive.

That was the theory. But often two or three months would go by before I received a packet, at which time I might be handed three of them, one, or a mostly empty envelope. Could have been inmates with a grudge working the mail room, some guard's petty meddling or arrogant notion of control, or it could have been just plain workaday pilferage. Never an explanation, of course, and you learned quickly, once those doors slammed shut behind you, never to question. Had it not been for the protection afforded me by fish-nor-fowl status and, later, by one teacher's taking an unwarranted interest, I'm sure the college soon would have scoured me from its pot. But it didn't. I'd gone into serious overdraft, but checks were still being cashed.

October of that second year, I received my M.A. The elaborate certificate, on heavy cream-colored bond replete with Gothic lettering and Latin, came rolled in a tube such as the ones in which other inmates received the *Barbarella,* Harley-Davidson and R. Crumb posters taped to the walls of their cells. University regents wished to inquire, an attached letter read, as to whether I would be continuing my education at their facility. Forever a quick study, having now survived inside and in addition found my way through thickets of university regulations, I felt as though I'd turned myself into some kind of facility veteran, slippery enough to slalom around raindrops, savvy enough to ride the system's thermals. Better the facility you know. You bet I will be, I told university regents.

If every year April comes down the hill like an idiot, babbling and strewing flowers, then October steps up to the plate glum and serious—never more than that one.

Lifting a pound or two of prison clothes off the counter, I'd picked up a ton of grief with them. That I'd been a cop was not supposed to get out. But guards knew, which meant everyone knew, and every one of them, inmates and guards alike, had good reason to despise the various shipwrecks that had cast them up here. They weren't able to slit society's neck or shove the handle of a plumber's helper up Warden Petit's rear end, but there *I* was. From the first, starting out small and escalating the way violence always does, I'd met with confrontations on the yard, at mealtime, in the showers, at workshop. Two months and half a dozen scrambles in, I received a rare invitation from Warden Petit himself—I hadn't been able to back off fast enough, and guards, looking away, had given me time to break the guy's jaw before moving in— who wanted to tell me how proud he was of the way I was handling myself.

"Thank you, Warden."

"Tremendous pressures on you out there. I appreciate that, you know. I see it. They never let up on a man, do they?" A triangular patch of hair had been left behind on his forehead as the rest withdrew. He made a show of consulting papers on the desk before him. "Like a cup of coffee?"

"No."

"Scotch?" His eyes came back up to mine. I'd been given a folding chair designed, apparently, for maximal discomfort.

Reminded me of the bunk and toilet in my cell.

"You're dripping blood on my floor." He keyed the intercom. "Get Levison in here," he said, then to me: "Don't worry," as he smiled. "We're used to it. And it's not really my floor, is it?"

Petit was like those guys who as hospital administrators a decade or so later would start calling themselves CEOs, wanting to live just a little large. He wore a light gray suit that made him resemble nothing so much as a block of cement with a head balanced atop. The head kept nodding and bobbing about like it wasn't placed well and might topple off any minute. Hope springs eternal.

"Absolutely not mine. It's the taxpayers' floor."

His personal floors, I had no doubt, would be scoured clean. By inmates or trustees if not by his own scab-kneed wife.

"You'd best get on down there. Medic's waiting for you at the infirmary."

I was almost through the door when he said: "Turner?"

I stopped.

"You're on good road. What, two months more? Don't let 'em skid you out. Do it easy."

"Do my best."

As I left, Levison, seventy-plus if he was a day, shuffled past me carrying bucket and mop. Squirt bottles and rags hung on his pants like artillery.

Next morning, this guy steps up to me in the shower. I see him coming, the shank held down along his leg, see the fix in his eyes. At the last moment I shove out my hand and swing the heel up hard. The shank, a sharpened spoon, pierces his chin, pins his tongue. He opens his mouth trying to talk and

I see the tongue flailing about in there, only the tip able to move as he slides down the shower wall.

Was that enough? Did I have to kill him? I don't know. At the time it seemed I'd been left no choice. Another homily, another of the commandments we live by, says once a man steps up to you, you have to put him down.

Neither did the courts feel *they* had much choice. In their hands my three-year sentence blossomed to twenty-five.

# Chapter Nineteen

"I SERVED EIGHT MORE YEARS, GOT another degree, in psychology, a master's again, and began thinking maybe I could make some kind of life out of that. What else did I have to build on? By the time early release came around, I knew I wanted to work as a therapist. I set up in Memphis, made the rounds of school social workers, doctor's offices, community centers and so on to introduce myself and leave business cards, started picking up clients. Slowly at first, and anybody who walked in. But I had some kind of real feel, an instinct, for the acutely troubled ones—those at the edge of violence. Within a year that's mostly who I was seeing."

Sheriff Bates was nigh the perfect listener. His eyes had never left me as he leaned back in his chair, making himself comfortable, wordlessly inviting me to go on. Then he propped it up: "You found work you were good at. Damn few of us are ever lucky enough to do that."

"I know, believe me. Knew it then."

"But you quit."

"After six years, yes."

He waited.

"I'm not sure I *can* explain." Where's a movie-of-the-week plot when you need one?

A mockingbird lit on the sill and peered in at us, chiding.

"That the one Don Lee took to feeding?" Bates asked.

Daughter June nodded.

"And you wouldn't have anything to do with that."

In what was apparently a longtime private joke, she batted eyelashes at him.

"Time when that girl was eleven, twelve, every week she'd show up after school with some kind of orphan or another. A kitten, puppy, a hatchling she claimed fell out of a tree, not much to it but a skull, feet and hungry mouth. Once, a baby rabbit—they say once those have the stench of human on them, parents seek them out and kill them.

"You'd best go ahead and feed the thing," he said after a moment, "else we'll never hear the end of it." Then to me: "You've done some hard wading against the current."

"Off and on."

"More on than off, from the sound of things. Work like what you ended up doing, that has to be like police work, demands a lot of you. And the better you are at it, the more it takes."

"True enough. Just being on the job, on the streets, not anything in particular that happened, made a difference. Changed me, damaged me: the point could be argued. All those years tramping around in other people's heads was a kind of repeat."

"Not to mention prison."

We watched June, outside, scatter birdseed on the sill and back away from it as the mockingbird returned. Glancing up at us, she waved.

"One day ostensibly like all others, sitting there with my morning coffee and appointment book, I looked out the window and realized the floors were gone. They'd just dropped out from under me, they were gone. I knew I no longer trusted anyone or anything. That I could see around, through and behind every motive—my own no less than everyone else's."

"So you decided to be alone."

"I'm not sure it was a conscious decision. How much of what's most important in our lives ever is?"

June came in and pulled her purse from an open desk drawer, saying she had to pick up Mandy at school, she'd drop her off and be right back.

"That time already, is it?" Bates said. And I, once she was gone, that I hadn't known June had a child.

"No reason you would. But she doesn't—not yet, anyway. Friend of hers, Julie, works as a nurse, twelve-hour shifts twice a week. June helps out. The two of them went right through school together, kindergarten on up, you couldn't pry 'em apart with a crowbar."

"June and Julie."

"Cute, huh?"

"Other kids must have had fun with that."

"Only the first time or two. You haven't seen it yet, but that girl has a temper'd make a grizzly back off, go home and call out for food."

"Someone else takes care of the child once she drops it off?"

"Julie's brother. Clif's not old enough to have his license yet, but he goes over after school and stays with Mandy till Julie gets home. Has dinner waiting most nights, too, I hear."

The phone rang.

"Sheriff B—"

He looked at me, shook his head.

"Yes ma'am, I—"

His end of the conversation was like a motor turning over again and again, never catching.

"Yes ma'am. If—"

"Yes ma'am. Can I—"

"What—"

He tugged a notepad towards him and scribbled something on the top page.

"We'll get right on that, ma'am," he said, then, hanging up, "Surprise you?"

It took a beat or two for me to realize the last comment was addressed to me, that he was referring to what he'd told me about June and the friend's baby.

"A little, Sheriff."

What I'd truly been thinking was whether I was still in the United States. This couldn't be the same country I saw reflected in news, TV shows, current novels. Mind you, I didn't watch TV or read newspapers and hadn't read a novel since prison days, but it all filtered in. Thoreau, Zarathustra, Philip Wylie's superman alone and impotent on his mountaintop—in today's world they'd all be aware what shows were competing for the fall lineup, the new hot fashion designer, the latest manufactured teen star.

But people watching over friends' children as though their own? A teenage brother taking responsibility for his sibling's child?

Bates tore off the note he'd just made and tipped it into the wastebasket.

"Time you dropped that 'Sheriff' business, don't you think? Friends call me Lonnie."

Five or six responses came to mind.

"Friend's a tough concept for me," I finally said.

"It'll come back to you." He smiled. "You like chicken?"

★ ★ ★

THREE HOURS LATER I FOUND MYSELF seated at an ancient, much-abused walnut dining table. My new best friend Sheriff Bates aka Lonnie sat at the head of the table to my right, wife Shirley directly across, June at the other end, a couple of teenage sons, Simon with a brush cut and baggies, Billy with multiple piercings dressed all in black, in the remaining chairs. Plate heaped with mashed potatoes, fried chicken. Bowls of stewed okra and tomatoes, milk gravy and corn on the cob placed around a centerpiece of waxed fruit in a bowl. Shallow bowl of chow-chow, small white bowls with magnolia blossoms afloat in water scattered about. Anachronistic platter of commercial brown-and-serve rolls. The TV sat like a beacon, sound dialed down, angled in, just past the connecting doorway to the living room. The boys' eyes never left it as Fran Drescher's nanny gave way to *Fresh Prince*.

"We're pleased you could join us," Shirley Bates said.

"Thank you for having me. The food's wonderful."

"Nothing fancy, I'm afraid."

"I don't know, the magnolias add a certain festive touch."

"You like them?" Pleasure lit her face. "Lonnie thinks they're silly. It's something my mother used to do."

Mine too—I'd just remembered that.

Afterwards, the sheriff and I helped stack dishes and take them out to the kitchen through a door propped open with a rubber wedge of a kind I hadn't seen in years. Declining offers of further assistance, Shirley said "You go play good host, honey. God knows you can use the practice. I'll finish up here."

Bates poured coffee from a Corningware percolator into mugs with pictures of sheep and deer. A sliding door opened directly from the kitchen onto a patio. Four or five white plastic chairs sat about, the grid inside a grill was caked with char above white ghosts of charcoal, jonquils sprang brightly from a small plot by the house. A rake leaned against the wall nearby, tines clotted with dark, brittle leaves. We sat chatting about nothing of substance, sequence or consequence. When a knock came at the wooden gate to the driveway, Bates called out: "Come on in."

He wore a dark blue suit whose double-breasted coat drained half an apparent foot or so off the actual height I encountered when I stood to shake hands. Around lower legs and cuffs were swaths of whitish-looking hair from a house pet, dog or cat. Leather loafers long neglected, a silk tie carefully knotted early that morning then forgotten.

"You must be Turner."

"Mayor Sims," Bates said as we shook hands.

"Henry Lee. Please. Thanks for having me by, Lonnie."

"Been way too long. And you'd best go in and pay respects to Shirley before you leave—if you know what's good for me."

"I will, I will."

"So why don't I go get drinks. Black Jack as usual, Henry Lee?"

"You have to ask?"

"Beer, if it's not too much trouble," I said.

"You've got it."

It took Bates a long while to get those drinks. A couple of times I saw him edging up to the kitchen window, looking out. I had little doubt he meant for me to see that.

"So," Mayor Sims said, sinking into a chair. "You going to be able to pull that layabout's butt out of the fire on this?"

"We'll see."

All about us, over by the house, near the gate, above a solitary fig tree, the cold chemical light of fireflies came and went.

"How's your mail delivery these days?" I asked.

"I have noticed a difference."

"Glad to hear it." I listened to mosquitoes spiraling in close by my ears. Whatever the reason, I'd never been much to their taste. They come in, do the research, apply elsewhere.

"I've been wondering how you were able to go three months without ever noticing no bills had been paid."

"Point taken." We watched a bat flap across moonlit sky. Scooping up gnats, mosquitoes and moths as it went, no doubt. *Joyful* is a human word, but it was hard to watch the bat's flight without its coming to mind. "My wife always took care of household bills, balanced the checkbook, all that. Anything needing my attention, something out of the ordinary, she'd let me know. Dorothy's in a nursing home. I put her there two weeks ago. Alzheimer's."

"I'm sorry."

"Took me a long time to admit to myself something was seriously wrong. A lot longer to admit it to others. Damn, I was getting forgetful myself, you know? Dorothy always hid it well. And when something did get past us and hit the wall, there I'd be, ready with an excuse for her. Besides, the way I was brought up—you too, would be my guess—whatever happens in the family, you handle it. You take care of your own."

Lonnie emerged with our drinks and the two of them made small talk for a few minutes, hunting seasons, local football, that sort of thing, before the mayor excused himself, stood, downed the remainder of his drink in a single swallow, and went inside. Moments later the mayor came out, said good-bye to the two of us, strode through the gate and was gone.

★ ★ ★

"WHAT D'YOU THINK?" Lonnie said.

"Other than that you set me up?"

Full night now. Fewer mosquitoes, and the cicadae had quietened. Deepening silence everywhere. Stars brightened, intense white as though tiny holes had been punched in a black veil, letting through the merest suggestion of some blinding light that lurked just past, waiting.

"Get you another?"

I held up my half-full bottle.

"I live here," Lonnie said. "Sometimes—"

"I understand."

"Man's full of himself. And I don't approve of a lot of what he does. Few years back, the city council passed an ordinance that rental houses had to have internal plumbing, bathrooms. How they pushed that past him I don't know, since he owns almost every unit of cheap housing in the county—all those plywood, used-lumber and tarpaper shacks south of downtown?"

I'd seen them. Hell, I'd grown up with their like.

"Toilets went in wherever it was easiest. In kitchens, bedrooms, on the porch. Crew had it all done within the week. I'm going to freshen this up. Sure you don't want another?"

He was back in moments but instead of resuming his seat stood looking off at the dark silhouettes of trees.

"He doesn't need me or anyone else to approve of what he does. I don't need that, either. Don't have to approve of him, I mean."

"I understand, Lonnie. I really do."

"He told you about Miss Dorothy?"

I nodded.

"Been coming a long time. We all saw it, long before he did. Some ways, I think it's changed him as much as it has her. Never had children, there's just the two of them. Man has to be lonely."

He sat again.

"Beautiful night."

I agreed, and we sat quietly side by side, listening to gushes of water from the kitchen as Shirley rinsed dishes. Somewhere close by, a bullfrog called.

"You miss the city? I know I asked you that before."

"The city, yes. But I don't miss the person I became in the city."

"He really that much different?"

I nodded.

"Not a good man? Sort of person you saw him coming, you'd cross the street?"

"Right."

"So here you are, this beautiful evening, miles away from any city at all, with a handful of new friends. Still trying to get across the street to avoid that man."

# Chapter Twenty

THE MOON HUNG ORANGE AS Halloween candy in the sky, a perfect circle that made the city's spinal ridge—single-level convenience stores, three- or four-story apartment and office buildings and high-rises all in a jumble—look even more eccentric, more unnatural. No right angles in nature. I remembered that from some all-but-forgotten art class.

On the seat beside me, Randy tipped back his head to squirt saline up his nose. Bottle the size Merthiolate used to come in when I was a kid and everyone called it monkey blood. Stuff was like dye. Get it on you, it was there till the skin sluffed away. Not a lot of plastic around then, though. Monkey blood came in glass bottles. You painted it on with a glass stinger attached to the cap. Plastic dinnerware started showing up when I was in grade school.

"You okay?" I said.

"I'm fine. Look: you have problems with the squad you pull, you take it back in, right? It doesn't corner, scrapes its way over potholes or bottoms out, maybe the mirrors are gone permanently cockeyed, you take it back in." He tucked the saline bottle away, staring straight ahead. "No different with a partner."

Despite rank, we'd been put on the streets in an unmarked car responding to general calls. Other detectives were first call; we were backup. Brass didn't trust Randy.

We turned onto Maple. Outside a Piggly Wiggly there, a girl of sixteen or so sat slumped against a *Press-Scimitar* coin box, knees up, head down. She'd tucked the garbage bag that was her luggage and held everything she owned under her legs. As I got out of the squad, six yards off, the smell of her hit me. I walked towards the notch of wasted pale thighs.

"You okay, miss?"

Her eyes swam up, found me. "What?"

"Are you okay?"

"I don't know. I *look* okay?"

I helped her to her feet. Reflexively one hand shot out to grab hold of the bag, which came up with her. She tottered, then straightened, found the fulcrum. Near as tall as myself.

"Not many gentlemen left."

"You have some place to go, miss?"

She thought a moment, shook her head.

"Then—"

"A sister," she told me. "West Memphis. Just across the bridge."

"Best get moving that way. Stick around here, sooner or later you're gonna get hauled in, or worse."

She levered the bag over one shoulder. "Thank you, Officer."

"No need to thank me. Just take care of yourself, miss."

"You too."

"Five blocks from here she'll forget where she was

heading," Randy said when I got back in the squad. "You know that."

"So—what? We take her in, she's back on the street tomorrow, nothing gained but a meal or two, some abuse if she's lucky, rape and a beating or two if she's not. We drop her off in ER, she gets a psych consult, who knows where that's going. Hard to imagine it'd be anyplace good."

We slowed to cruise a line of shopfronts, independent insurance companies, a travel agent, a used-clothing store, that sort of thing, then pulled around to the alley, an occasional favorite of local teenagers on the prowl, and ran that.

"It's the medication," Randy said as we pulled back into traffic. Cross streets ticked by. Walnut Street, left onto Vance across Orleans. "Dries you out something fierce."

Able north past Beale and Union.

All told, an uneventful shift. We pulled in at the station house with half an hour to spare, only routine paperwork outstanding, no mandatories to clear. Randy and I sat in the break room. He was filling out the shift report, I was drinking coffee. Sixth cup of the day? He pushed the form across the table for me to countersign. The rest of the shift's warriors had begun streaming in by then, clapping backs and telling new war stories, stowing uniforms in lockers (some of them, the uniforms, a little smelly, sure, but dry cleaning's expensive), splashing water on armpits, chest, neck and face at the bank of four narrow sinks in the communal washroom, smearing deodorant underarm, spritzing on cologne or nipping from flasks before heading out to rejoin the world as citizens.

As though they could.

I'd changed into jeans and a sweatshirt, my gray

windbreaker. Pockets were long gone, the zipper was trying hard to follow, collar frayed half through. I went down the two steps the station house thought it needed to set itself apart from its surround, around the corner to the parking lot. I was just climbing into my truck, which looked a lot like the windbreaker, when Randy's head bobbed up alongside.

"Anywhere you need to be?"

"Not really."

"So maybe we could get a beer or two."

So we did, four in fact, in the lounge of a Holiday Inn nearby. Waitresses kept straying through from the restaurant to see if we wanted to order food. Out in the lobby a guy played piano, great rolling flourishes shaped with both hands like snowballs around rocks of five-, six-note melodies: tonic, dominant, subdominant, home. Barest kiss of the relative minor. In one back booth a man sat speaking intently with a woman half his age. His eyes never left hers. Hers never met his.

"Look, you know how the projectionist doesn't get the film focused just right, it's a blur?" Randy told me over the second beer. "You keep looking away and looking back, thinking it's gonna come clear. Like there's two pictures, two worlds, half an eyeblink apart. Then you take the meds and it all comes together, the blur goes away."

Maybe (I remember thinking even then) the blur is what it's all about.

We sat there quietly, glancing vaguely at clips from football games and wrestling on the TV above the bar as the doors from the lobby opened to admit a wheelchair. It came in backwards. Having no foot panels, it was propelled and directed by the occupant's swollen, bandaged feet. Watching in the rearview mirror mounted on one armrest, that occupant made his way into the lounge. Around his neck was what looked to be a twisted coat hanger. It held a kind of panpipe into which the occupant blew as he advanced, to warn of his passage. Possibly his arms, his upper body, were paralyzed?

But no, as he reached the bar and turned his chair about, the bartender handed across a glass of draft beer.

"How's it going, Sammy?"

The man took a long pull off the beer before answering. "Not bad. Could be worse. Has been, lots."

"Check came in on time, I see."

"Day late."

"Not a dollar short too, I hope."

Sammy's features drew together in what was obviously a laugh. His shoulders heaved. There was little sound to the laugh, and tears came out his eyes. After a moment he leaned forward to put the empty glass on the bar. The bartender had a replacement waiting. Sammy drank it almost at a gulp and put it on the bar beside the first. Shifting weight onto his right haunch, he tugged free a wallet.

The bartender waved away his effort. "This one's on me."

"You sure?"

"Sure I'm sure."

"Thanks, bud. 'Preciate it."

"Take care, friend."

Sailor Sammy tacked the wheelchair around and, puffing on his panpipe, started backwards towards the door.

"Wet his whistle," Randy said to the bartender as he came back from opening the door.

"He did that all right. Get you another?"

"Why the hell not."

I nodded.

He brought them.

"Boy comes in every week, sometimes Monday, sometimes Tuesday. Has two beers like you just seen. Flat downs them, then he's gone. Don't have any idea what this check is he's always talking about—welfare, some kinda government thing—but he flat won't come in till it gets there. Not that I've ever taken his money."

"You know him?" Randy asked.

"Not really. Lives in a garage out behind someone's house, I think. Maybe up Fannin Street way, just off Pioneer? Somewhere in there."

"What happened to him?" Randy asked.

The bartender shrugged, shoulders rising momentarily from a tier of low-end vodkas and gins to one of call Scotches and subsiding.

"You've done a mitzvah," I said.

The bartender looked at me as Randy grinned. 'Round those parts, those days, Judaism was as exotic as artichokes. I may as well have brought up Masonic rites, alchemy, the pleasures of goat cheese.

Doors from the lobby again swung open, this time to admit a party of office workers, six of them, in ill-fitting dresses and suitcoats with something of the oxbow about them, stiff plastic ties, costume jewelry, run-over shoes thick with bottled polish. From the back table where they settled, quickly their presence spilled out into the room, taking it over. As though in stop-time, suddenly the table was awash with empty bottles and glasses, cigarette packets, purses, ashtrays.

On TV, wrestlers Sputnik Malone and Billy Daniels took elaborate turns throwing one another about the ring. Memphis wrestling had been big for years and still drew huge crowds. It was televised locally; during the week, stars like Malone and Daniels toured the mid-South, wrestling in high-school gymnasiums, American Legion posts and Catholic clubs.

Sitting there, I noticed that while good paneling sheathed the walls and carpets shrouded floors, such refinements ended at the bar itself, undeveloped country with bare floors behind, sketchy shelves, squares of wood nailed to cabinets and drawers for pull handles. Bare wires hung from holes in the ceiling.

A basket of cheese cubes, cut-up pickles and bologna, all of them speared with toothpicks, appeared before us. I glanced over at the office workers' table. Three baskets there. Another half-dozen set out. Remains of the limb of a sizeable tree here in the room with us. Slivered. Julienned.

"Gentlemen?" the bartender asked.

Randy doubled him: "One for the road?"

I glanced at my watch—just as though I had somewhere to go.

"Sure."

For a time then, silently, we worked at the new drinks. Wrestling gave way to a local talent show, all but one of the contestants female and a fair divide among singers, baton twirlers and those offering dramatic recitations. The male tap-danced.

"You don't trust me," Randy said.

Falling back on the facile and hating myself for it: "I'm not sure you trust yourself."

"Two different things, though, aren't they?" His eyes found my face in the mirror behind the bar. "I love you, man. You know that."

I nodded.

I took that thought home with me and, half an hour later, soaking in a tub of hot water, nodded again. Country music drifted in softly from the bedroom, voices from next door came to visit through thin walls, and from the street through open windows, traffic swooshed and hooted beyond. In silent toast I held up my glass and watched the bathroom's light turn gold. I drank then, eyes shut, eyes behind which, perhaps in their own quiet way growing impatient, dreams waited.

Grace be with us all, who are so alone and lost.

# Chapter Twenty-One

GRACE IS TOUGH GAME TO BRING down. Sputnik Malone or Plato, either would be hard put to pin it. Most of us are lucky if we so much as catch a glimpse of the thing our whole lives—its back, maybe, as it hurries away through the crowd. I remembered the prodigy Raymond Radiguet. *In three days' time I will be shot to death by the soldiers of God.*

Val had brought Carl Hazelwood's notebook back to us two days before. Nothing much of forensic interest, she said. Techs had what they needed, manufacturer, item, batch numbers, all that, they'd be following up. Our own files contained photocopies of notebook pages, and I'd been through them a dozen times at least. We all had. But something about having in my hands the actual, much-abused, saddle-worn artifact drew me to it, and I sank in again. Not that anything had changed. Not that I had new information, new understanding or insight. Or the paltriest clue as to what might be going on.

It was one of those huge five-subject notebooks, sections divided by heavy inserts, doubled coils of wire at the spine. Two lines of obsessively neat script ran right up to page edge on either side between scored blue lines. A thousand words per page, at least. Most early entries had faded away, now only blurred cuneiform, ranks of diminutive Rorschachs, make of it what you will or can. Elsewhere ink had given up the ghost entirely, dissolving into pools of wash, like watercolor.

*Dad told me the stew was good. I had it waiting when he got home. We talked a little bit afterward, then It Came from Outer Space was on TV. When dad came in I was wiping up spills off the floor with one of his shirts. It was dirty already so I don't understand why he got so mad. Maybe I ought to put more celery in next time. He looks like my uncle, sure he does, but he's not. That's from the movie.*

————

*I was sitting outside this morning and a cat came up to me, orange all over, even its eyes. It came up and rubbed against the step where I was, kind of half falling down, but every time I tried to touch it it ran off. Then a minute or two later it'd come back. I pinched off a piece of bologna and held it out. Mr. Cat liked that. He'd dodge in and grab hold, then go off under some bushes to eat. Mr. Cat ate most of a sandwich that way. Finished off the bread myself.*

————

*Found a cache of magazines in the basement in a box under some empty suitcases. Since the top of the box was filled with old newspapers I almost didn't look any further, but there they were underneath. A stack of Popular Mechanics, two years of Scientific Americans, a bunch of Astoundings and Fantastics crumbling at the*

*bottom. Guess bugs must like those. One of the Popular Mechanics
had a piece on building your own electric car, diagrams, specs, the
whole works, even where you could order parts. Read most of a
story by Fredric Brown, but the last two pages were missing.*

————

*Wrote a long letter to Sydney. I really miss her. I'd copy it down
here, but my hand hurts. Anyway, it's already in the mail and gone.
I looked up Minnesota in the encyclopedia. They put electric
blankets inside their car hoods. There are lakes everywhere. Cissie
says she checked and where Sydney went is a good place. They'll
take good care of her there, Cissie says. Someone will read your
letter to her. I hope she remembers me. It's been a long time. You do
understand, don't you, Cissie said. She just got so she needed more
taking care of than her mom and dad and her family could handle.
Sure I did. I watched it happen. I even remember wondering if that
could happen to me, if maybe someday I'd get like that, get lost the
way Sydney did and have to go away.*

————

*Oatmeal for breakfast. Bacon, lettuce and tomato with lots of
mayonnaise for lunch. The rest of the meat loaf, turnip greens,
roasted sweet potatoes and ice tea for dinner. A good day. I even got
a letter! From a pen pal in Finland. I found his name and address
in the back of an old magazine. He was fourteen when he placed
the ad, he wrote, and he's amazed that my letter found him. It had
been forwarded through three addresses. Now he's a history professor
at a university, has a wife and two daughters. Finland sounds a lot
like Minnesota.*

――――

*The social worker we'd been waiting for came this morning, just like in A Thousand Clowns. There was white stuff all over the front of her blue sweater and long hairs on the back, her own and a cat's I think, and she smelled like sour milk. Afterwards she and Dad talked out in the kitchen. I got the door for her and watched as she hobbled off down the hall, thinking how much she looked like Piper Laurie in The Hustler, right up to the limp. The limp's a kind of badge, I guess. Maybe they even teach it in social worker school. I'M ONE OF YOU.*

――――

*Jack Finney's book was a disappointment after Invasion of the Body Snatchers. On the other hand, Evan Hunter's novel of Blackboard Jungle was much better—no contest, really. Right next to it on the shelf was Streets of Gold, so I picked that one up too, and it's my new favorite. I've read it half a dozen times by now. The writer publishes as Hunter and as Ed McBain, neither of which is his real name, which is Salvatore Lombino. He also wrote the screenplay for The Birds. I couldn't make much more sense out of O'Hara's novel of Butterfield 8 than I did the movie.*

Whole pages were filled with pasted-in receipts for magazines and paperbacks, lunches at McDonald's, Good Eats cafeteria and Poncho's, city bus transfers, cash tickets listing writing tablets, athletic socks, hard candy and breakfast cereals, verses and scrawled signatures scissored from greeting cards, ragged entries torn from TV Guides.

"Come across something there?" Don Lee asked, dredging

me back, salvaged. I'd been quite literally out of this world, feet planted squarely in Carl Hazelwood's, a world that made a lot more sense than our own. I was a visitor there, of course, a tourist, nothing more. Rare enough for any of us to be able to manage even that. But I'd become an old hand at looking through others' windows from inside. In a way that's how I survived prison. More to the point, it's what made me effective as a therapist. And why I'd stopped.

I got up, dumped last night's leftovers from the coffeemaker, scrubbed cone and carafe, found a filter, put on a fresh pot.

"Ever consider coming on full-time, you've got my vote," Don Lee said.

"I do a mean grilled cheese, too."

He sighed dramatically.

Adrienne picked up on the fourth ring, breathing hard.

"Turner," I said. "Not calling too early, I hope."

"Not at all. We're used to short nights. Dad always tries to hold still as long as he can so as not to disturb us, but he doesn't sleep much. Two or three hours at the most. Good days, he's able to fall back asleep around dawn."

The coffeemaker burbled. A raked pickup with glass packs and booming bass blew past outside. When the phone rang, Don Lee punched in the other line and picked up, from old habit pulling a pad of paper close. June would be in soon. For a half-hour or so the street would be busy. If I stepped outside now, I'd emerge into congeries of smells: toast and bacon and coffee from the diner, car exhaust and unburned gasoline, cheap unbottled perfume of magnolia, newly watered front yards.

"Sarah's out running," Adrienne said. "I'd had enough, but

she thought she'd go on a bit, should be back soon. Shall I have her call you?"

As one ages, signs that the world has changed at first appearance are subtle. One day you realize you've lost touch with music, don't have a clue what this new stuff's all about. Then the cops start looking like teenagers. You sleep again and wake to a world you scarcely recognize. Running, for instance. Suddenly everyone's doing it. Everyone's working out at Bally's or L.A. Fitness, clinging to the sides of cliffs in day-long climbs, stoking yogurt, power shakes and smoothies like firemen in ancient railroad engines. What the hell's happened?

"You may be able to help," I told Adrienne.

"All right."

Across the room Don Lee said, "We'll look into it, Bonnie... Right... I've got it all written down here... Right..."

"You all getting along okay out there?" I asked.

"We're adaptable, Mr. Turner, always have been. Making do is where we live." Upturning a bottle of water, she drank. I heard each segment of the process, from unscrewed cap through glugs to the bottle coming back upright. "What was it you wanted?"

Don Lee said: "Any questions, anything comes up, I'll give you a call."

"Who's BR?"

"Beg your pardon?"

"BR. It keeps coming up in Carl's notebook, more and more as time goes on."

"A friend, maybe?"

"His barber, for all I know. A pen pal, maybe?"

"I don't think I—hold on."

Voices off, as the phone changed hands.

"You come up against any more trouble like that, you give us a call right away," Don Lee said, disentangling with a sigh and setting the phone down.

"Mr. Turner?"

"Have a good run?"

"Remember what Woody Allen said about sex? The worst he ever had was wonderful?"

"Chasing endorphins."

"I'm sorry?"

"Supposedly they come to you when you push yourself to the limit. I ran for years, smacked up against my limit more than a few times. But I never so much as caught sight of the back end of one single endorphin."

Don Lee poured coffee for us both, set mine before me. I nodded thanks. He sat back down. Attending to his cross-word-puzzle book from the look of it.

"Did you have something for me, Mr. Turner?"

"Only a question, I'm afraid... Carl seems to have felt the same way about movies that you feel about running. Or Woody Allen about sex."

She laughed. "He did! And he loved the bad ones best of all. Like those old science fiction and horror movies he grew up on, godawful stuff. Herschell Gordon Lewis, Jack Arnold, Larry Cohen. *Basket Case, Spider Baby, The Incredibly Strange Creatures.* A lot of them had something about them, though, awful as they were. Some basic integrity, a personal vision."

"He talked about them a lot?"

"All the time. At least one of his therapists became exasperated. Said the kind of movies Carl was drawn to

141

merely objectified his paranoia."

"So would the *Congressional Record*."

Laughter again. "Creatures from lagoons, lost worlds and outer space are a lot more fun."

"Not to mention every bit as believable."

The door opened to let June slip through smiling. I noticed she kept her face turned away, and when she took her place at the front desk I understood why. That left eye was a prize of a shiner.

"Did Carl have particular favorites? Movies, actors, directors?"

"You know he was kind of a savant, right? Wherever his attention fell, it set down hard. He was like a sponge that would only soak up certain liquids. I remember one day we were talking in the kitchen and this song came on the radio, 'You Better Move On.' A week later he was telling me all about this obscure singer Arthur Alexander, his handful of hits, his comeback attempt with an album of autobiographical songs. God knows how or where he found out about all this stuff."

"Same with movies, I take it."

"Exactly. He could go on for hours about what studio put them out, where they were shot, who wrote the stories and scripts, how they set up this or that scene. He'd quote whole chunks of what Robert Mitchum or Brian Keith had said in *Thunder Road* or whatever. 'Bullet through the chest, ma'am, just routine'—that was one of his favorites. He absolutely worshiped Richard Carlson."

She paused, said, presumably to Adrienne, *"Please,"* then to me: "Here's a man who wouldn't use newfangled things like coffeepots, walked on the other side of the room to avoid microwaves, slept on the floor often as not, wore clothes till they dissolved around him, ran in terror from ringing telephones. But movies, he couldn't give up. When he left this last time, looking for any clue what might have happened, where he'd gone, we came across stacks of books out in the garage, had to be close to a hundred of them, behind cans of Valvoline and hand cleaner that looked like gray putty. Books with titles like *Forgotten Horrors, Truly Strange Movies, Grindhouse Fare.* They'd been taken from libraries all over the Midwest. Cedar Rapids and Iowa City, Dubuque, Chicago, Minneapolis, Cincinnati."

"Checked out?"

"Liberated. He didn't have cards, couldn't have got them."

"So he hadn't just wandered off, all those times. Some of them, anyway. He'd gone out there purposefully, into the wide world, to find and bring back those books."

"His treasure. Excuse me a moment, Mr. Turner."

The receiver clunked hollowly onto what I assumed to be a pressboard desktop. Briefly I heard footsteps receding; for a while, nothing at all; then she was back.

"I apologize. Dad's doing poorly this morning, I'm afraid. Can you tell me: should it become necessary, to what hospital should we take him?"

Expressing my concern, I told her there was a county hospital a bit less than an hour away on the interstate. But for anything serious she'd probably want to head to Memphis or Little Rock.

"Just in case," Miss Hazelwood said. "We're not there yet… What?" Words off. "Nor do we expect to be, Adrienne says I should tell you."

"That's good."

Don Lee held up his cup. More? I shook my head. Momentarily June's eyes met mine. She looked down.

"But who or what," I asked Sarah Hazelwood, "is BR?"

"Not a clue, I'm afraid."

"Okay. Thank you for your time. And listen, if your father—"

"Should we need anything, I promise I'll call."

Downing one last swallow of coffee, Don Lee stood, stretched, and headed out for afternoon patrol. June and I sat looking at one another. We heard the unit's door slam, heard the motor start and catch. Then the low whine of gears as Don Lee backed away. The radio crackled.

"You want to tell me about it?" I asked her.

"Not really," she said.

# Chapter Twenty-Two

SO GODDAMN ALONE AND LOST. Not my words but those of my final cellmate, Adrian.

Years later, Lonnie Bates would accuse me of expending too much energy distancing myself from the man I'd been. Maybe he was right, maybe I'd always be trying to get away from that man. Just like a part of me would always be in that prison cell, or another part sitting with a man's head in my lap, leaning over him as bright blood ran down the street in the rain. Just as a part of me would forever be standing there over the partner I'd just shot.

Amazing how static memory is, most of our lives gathered around a handful of tableaux.

Adrian once told me about African musicians he used to play with. When things became too predictable, too worked out, too repetitious, they'd exhort their fellows to "put some confusion in it."

I've never been able to describe what it was like to kill a man. Remembering the act itself is easy. There he is three showerheads down, makeshift knife held along his leg, now he's walking up to me, now he's stepping back, trying to talk with tongue pinned to the roof of his mouth, but what come out are animal sounds. All this is vivid. Vivid for him too, I'm sure, momentarily, these last few moments of his life. There has to be something of weight and substance here, some revelation, you think, there just *has* to be. But there isn't. You watch the light drain away behind his eyes, you look around to see who's witnessed this, you get up and go on. You've learned nothing. Death makes no more sense than any of the rest of it. You're alive. He's not. *That's* what you know.

Cellmate Adrian was a fortyish man of ambiguous ethnicity, Caucasian, Negroid and Asian-Amerind features all boiled down together in the pot. He liked to refer to himself as octoroon. "Has to be lots more roons than that mixed up in me," he'd say, "but eight's high as they go, back home." Back home was New Orleans. Sexually, too, he was a puzzle: chocky, muscled frame and a hard, square stride, arms and hands moving fluidly when he spoke, an up-from-under glance. This had ceased being a topic of conversation his fifth week in. One of those who'd seen fit to remark it had a skull permanently deformed, soft as a melon rind, from the time Adrian came upon him with six batteries (taken from appliances and tools in the workshop) knotted into a pillowcase.

"Hear tell you're a cop," he said to me our first night together. I'd had a couple cellmates before him. Neither had lasted long.

"Not anymore. Not a lot of cops in here, I'd guess."

He laughed. "Not enough room for those that should be."

A guard walked the rows, dragging his baton lightly across bars to forewarn us of his coming.

"Man you killed, he was a friend?" Adrian said once the guard passed.

"Yes."

"Don't seem surprised I know that."

"I grew up in a small town."

"Small town. Yeah, that's what this is, all right."

Two or three cells down, a man sobbed.

"Poor son of a bitch," Adrian said. "Every goddamn night. Could be *you*'ll do all right in here, though. What's your name, boy?"

He had to know already, but I told him. Populated entirely by those unable to adapt to society's laws or societal norms, prisons have unspoken codes of etiquette such as to put tradition-bound southerners, Brits or Japanese to shame.

"Adrian," he said, "but most ever'one calls me Backbone. Tend to pick our name hereabouts, or if we don't, get 'em picked for us. In here, we're not what the world made us anymore. Long as you can back it up, you're what you say you are. Best get to sleep now. Sleep's just 'bout th'only friend you got here." Turning on his side, he breathed deeply. "'Cept me." And that quickly he was snoring.

There in the box that's become your home and second body, every small sound takes on unreasonable weight. Rake of the guard's baton along bars, ragged breath of the man on the bunk below, conversations stealing in from adjacent cells or those across the block, coughs ricocheting from wall to wall.

With a sound like a novice's first attempt at notes on a French horn, someone farts, and someone else laughs. Voices zigzag along the block in response.

"Okay, who smuggled perfume aboard?"

"Hey, he just sendin' flowers to his honey is all."

"Big boo-kay a stinkweed, more like it."

147

"Some brothers *like* that brown perfume."

"Donchu be talking 'bout no brothers over there, boy."

"Yassuh!"

"I meant like big brothers."

"Sure you did."

"Why'n't you all just shut th'fuck up and go to sleep."

Which is what that same voice said every night, and what finally happened.

Three walls of the cell, then another wall. Imagine your way past one wall, there's another, then another. We live in them, in the hollows and crawl spaces, like rats. The walls are what's important. We're what's not, though the walls are here because of us.

"Might dole up s'more roughage for my man here," Adrian said the next day in lunch line, "boy's new to the game." Another gloppy spoonful of cabbage hit my tray. "Good man," he told the inmate serving. "You'll be remembered."

"Move along," the server said. "Fuck off and die too, while you're at it." Hair buzzed to an eighth-inch, sleeves rolled above cable-like biceps, some kind of home-cooked tattoo there, a scorpion, maybe.

That's when I saw it for the first time. Adrian went dead still, face blank as the walls about us.

"You got somethin' to say to me back there, tattoo man?"

Briefly the server's eyes met Adrian's. Then he cast them about like a fisherman's net. Being in control of mashed potatoes and lima beans wasn't going to help him much. Nothing was. Not even his tattoo.

"Sorry," the server said. "Been a bad day. You know."

"Ain't they all?"

We moved along the line.

"Motherfuckers call themselves a brotherhood."

"White supremacists, you mean."

He nodded. "They be getting in touch witchu soon enough, I reckon."

"Damn," I said, trying my best to sound like Adrian. "All *kind* of scum in here, ain'there?"

He laughed. "There is, for sure."

It was a couple of weeks later that they came for me, two of them edging out around the massive dryers on a day I'd been assigned laundry duty.

"You and big nigger been gettin' on all right?" one asked. He had to shout to be heard above the dryers. From talk on the yard I knew him as Billy D. Barely topping five feet, he looked like steel wire braided into human form. Sleeves split to give biceps room.

Anything you say in these situations usually serves only to make it worse, so I didn't answer, just stood waiting. See how it comes down. Four or five more of what I assumed to be sworn members of the brotherhood shuffled into place. Two behind Billy D, two or three behind me.

"You're a white man, Turner. One of us."

I watched him, waiting for the body shift, the change in posture or expression that would signal we were taking it up a notch.

"Maybe you like that big dick of his so much, you just plain forgot that."

Then: "Not much for talking, are you?"

Inmates were expected to cringe in fear at Billy D's approach. That I hadn't, that in fact I'd shown nothing at all, unsettled his lackeys. Seeing that, he knew he had to lean in hard.

"You join us, Turner," he said. "Here. Today."

"No thanks."

Above and all about us, dryers rumbled. They were the size of the tumblers on cement trucks.

"What, you think you have some kinda choice?"

"Like you say, he's not much for talking."

All heads turned as the speaker stepped into the space between Billy D and myself. I knew him from talk on the yard. Angel. Looking around, I saw that each of Billy's lackeys by the wall had been flanked as well, two by blacks, one by an elegant Thai called Soon, three others by the 300-pound Samoan whose name seemed to be composed entirely of L's and gulps.

"We all got choices, white bread," Angel said. "How yours lookin' to you right now?"

Currents of fire and ice slammed back and forth. Ice won. Nodding, Billy D backed off a few steps, turned and left. As he did so, his men faded away too, then Angel's. Within moments I stood there alone.

"It's not over," Adrian said later when I tried to thank him. "You know that. May take a while, but they'll be back."

The day the guy came at me in the shower with the knife, I knew he was right.

# Chapter Twenty-Three

"I TOLD DADDY I GOT IT playing softball."

"And he believed you."

"Probably not. He did ask when I'd started playing softball. He … Well, you've gotten to know my father, you know it would take a lot for him to—what's the word I'm looking for?"

"Trespass?"

"I guess." For the first time, her face met mine straight on. "How bad does it look?"

"Purple's on your color chart, right?"

"I feel so …"

"Ashamed?"

"Stupid."

"You know you shouldn't."

"Of course I do."

A kid's face appeared in the window. Pushing against the glass, the boy pugged his nose, stuck out his tongue so that it too flattened, and crossed his eyes. Without benefit of the window, June returned a remarkable likeness of his caricature. He grinned and, mounting his skateboard like the Silver

Surfer, sped away. I had the sense they'd done this before.

"Anyhow, he's gone," June said.

"This is someone you cared for?"

She nodded.

"I'm sorry."

"Me too."

I fought your impossible war, America. I came back from it and for eight years as a cop, day in and day out, I witnessed the worst you and your citizens could do to one another. Then for almost as long I lived in the heads of some of those we—you and I—had most damaged. When I say her smile would break your heart, I mean it.

"I miss him," June said.

The phone rang.

"Sheriff's… Yes, ma'am… That's out by the Zorik place, right? … Right… We'll send a deputy right out."

Putting the phone down with a shrug of apology, she picked up the radio mike and keyed it on.

"Don Lee, you there?"

*Ten-four.*

"See the woman, third house off the gravel road half a mile past Fifty-one and Ledbetter."

*Near the old Zorik farm. Pecan orchard?*

"Right."

*Complaint?*

"Says her boy's back. Been snaring and killing her chickens for food but won't talk to her or let her get near him. ETA?"

*I'm halfway there already, out by the town dump. Twenty minutes, tops.*

"I'll call back, let her know."

"When I was a kid," I said once she'd done so, "my first real girlfriend, her family had a cousin living with them. From about twenty or so, life had turned into this steep downhill slide for him. Started out as assistant manager for one of the biggest clothing stores thereabouts and wound up doing janitor work at the elementary school—till he got fired from that. His own family threw him out once they found him in the baby's room standing over the crib. My girlfriend's mother took him in. Cissie and I'd be sitting watching TV, look up, and there he'd be, standing by the stove talking to it, or following the cat around the house from room to room for hours."

"Velma's boy hasn't been right since he turned twelve. Court keeps sending him away. Halfway houses, training schools, the state hospital. Sooner or later they let him go, or he runs off, and he shows up back here. Lives up in the hills mostly. Has to be all of thirty-five, forty now."

"None of us ever get too far from the cave."

"What happened?" June asked after a moment.

"Just what's supposed to happen. I went off to college, wrote long, passionate letters back almost daily. By the second semester I noticed I was getting fewer and fewer, ever briefer responses."

"I meant with the cousin."

"Oh… Well, one night, Ben was his name, one night Ben managed to get the latch off the porch door and wandered away. Next morning my girlfriend's mother was backing out of the drive, looking around hoping to see Ben or some sign of him, and ran over her infant son, my girlfriend's little brother."

"He make it?"

"Depends on your definition. He lived."

"Are you always so upbeat, Mr. Turner?"

"You caught me on a good day."

"Lucky me." She leaned forward to turn the radio on. Something ostensibly country, but worlds away from Riley Puckett or Ralph Stanley. "Get many dates, do you?"

"Enough."

"Out on the limb here, I'm gonna guess they're mostly first dates."

We sat together quietly. The phone rang. June answered, listened a moment and hung up. *I've looked and looked in all the bars, all the old places*—from the radio, spearchucker guitar behind.

"Sarah's a fine-looking woman."

"She is."

"You see anything happening there?"

"Happening?"

"Between the two of you."

"A little late in the game for that. When you're young, every chance encounter holds a bounty of possibilities. Pay for a six-pack at the 7-Eleven and this spark jumps up between you and the woman behind the counter. You think that'll go on happening forever."

June nodded.

"It doesn't. Before you know it, that's become the fantasy it always was, really. Someone's pulled the drawstring on the big grab bag. Everything's turned to wallpaper."

"I'm no expert, but you look to have, oh, I don't know, at least a good year or two left in you."

Both of us laughed.

"You worked as a therapist, Daddy says. Helping people figure out things like that for themselves."

"There never was a lot to figure out. Ninety-nine times out of a hundred, people understand perfectly well what's going on. They know what's right, what they need, why they do things the way they do."

*Hard as I looked, no one looked like you.*

"The majority of my clients went dutifully about lives and jobs. Many were exceptional at what they did. But, to the man, inside they were twisted, contorted, in pain—a chorus line of Quasimodos. Whether the wounds were real or not finally didn't matter, only their belief in those wounds. I'd kick back and listen. Sometimes I'd tell them how when you hear a good jazz guitarist you think he knows something the rest of us don't, that he understands how things connect, but he doesn't, it's just that he's honed this one small, special skill he has. He's got a hundred ways to get from here to there, sure. But the single most important thing he knows is simply to keep fingers and mind moving."

All around us, the town's gone still. From time to time the phone rings or the radio crackles into life.

"Your father tell you anything else?"

June shook her head. "Not really. I know you were a detective, of course."

So, with no real reason to do so, just that it seemed right at the time, I told her everything. My undeclared war, Memphis streets, Randy, prison and Backbone—all of it. Amazing how little space a life takes up, finally. That it should fit in so small an envelope.

When I was done, she sat silently a moment before saying, "This calls for *good* coffee, for a change." Minutes later, a kid's delivered from the diner and we're sipping the result. "We have an arrangement," June told me when I tried to pay.

"Your father know about this?"

"Sheriff Lonnie? That's what people call him around here, you know. Buy him a tank for his birthday if they thought he wanted one. Sure he knows. Sheriff Lonnie knows everything. He just doesn't approve of much of it."

"You included?"

June peered over the rim of her mug. "I'm bad," it read. She shrugged. The phone rang and, as though continuing the shrug, a single, extended motion, she picked up.

"Hi, Daddy... Quiet so far. Velma's boy's back again... Usual, sounds like. Don Lee's on his way out there... I'm fine... No... No."

"What the hell," I said, staring out the window.

A caravan of ancient trucks, cars and station wagons paraded down Main Street. As with covered wagons in westerns, belongings—furniture, housewares, pots and pans, boxes, what looked to be bedrolls—were lashed onto truck beds and the tops of vans and peeked from beneath car trunks lashed shut with rope.

"Gypsies just got here, Daddy... You said they'd be early this year, guess you were right... Old Meador place again? ... They'll leave it clean, at least..."

"They used to come with the carnival," June told me, hanging up. "They'd have rides that went up like Erector sets, games of skill, food stalls, maybe a freak tent, belly dancers, muscle men. Afternoons they'd descend on the town. Go into stores and while one of them paid for twine or a washboard at the front counter, others helped themselves to merchandise. They'd move door to door selling jewelry and hand-dyed cotton skirts and meat pies and when they were gone folks would find things missing, a gilded statue here, a humidor or crystal goblet there.

"Once the carnivals petered out, the gypsies kept coming, year after year, like robins and hummingbirds. But the carney mentality—the excuse of it?—passed with the carnivals. Now they kept to themselves, wouldn't think of going into homes. Two or three of them would show up in town, shop for staples at local stores, pay cash and hurry off."

"The code had changed."

"Right."

"If they're anything, gypsies are testaments to the adaptability of tradition, how you change to stay the same."

"You think about that a lot? The way things were, how you've changed to go along?"

She had something of her father's knack for staying quiet and waiting, like men on deer stands. Maybe she'd learned it from him. Or maybe she was just naturally a good listener. That very quality in her could attract men with baggage, the kind of men whose shrouded pain gradually congealed to abuse of one kind or another, emotional, physical. I'd seen it often enough before.

Though maybe I should stop reading so much into simple things.

I remembered all too well the smugness of therapists to whom I'd been subjected and others whom, later, I understudied. So many of them proceeded as though personalities were like Chinese menus, one from column A, one from column B, same few sauces for dish after dish, just different additives, give us ten minutes, no secret here. Early along I swore to myself—one of the few covenants I've kept—that I'd resist such an approach with every resource I possessed. Upon occasion this decision made me effective. Just as often, I fear, it rendered me worthless. But instinctively I swerved from that cocksure, mechanistic, reductive attitude whenever I saw it coming: knew it would diminish me as surely as it did my clients.

"I don't mean to pry, Mr. Turner," June said.

Don Lee's voice interposed itself, foot in the door, between radio crackles.

*June, you there?*

"Ten-four, Don Lee."

*Heard from the sheriff?*

"Just."

*Need him out here, now.*

"You still at Velma's?"

*Affirmative.*

"He'll be asking me why."

*Tell him I found Velma's boy trussed up in the shed back of the house. The chickens have been at him. They've done a good job. Got most of the good parts.*

# Chapter Twenty-Four

"WORD IS, YOUR TICKET'S GETTING punched," Backbone said.

I was up for a hearing the next morning.

"Maybe."

"No maybe to it. Done deal."

His hand came over the edge of the bed. I took and unfolded the sheet of paper it held.

"Two, three days' work there at the most, way I figure. You're not bound, you know. To any of it."

I looked. Messages I was asked to convey to wives, children, parents, companions, friends. A locker key to be picked up and passed along. Two or three other minor errands. Not at all unusual for departing inmates to carry wish lists like this out into the world with them. I told him it was all okay.

"No problem with that last one?"

A classic hat job. And for Billy D no less, the man who'd first marshaled his cronies against me in the laundry room. Now he was asking me to reach out to the partner who'd betrayed him, a partner who'd made it safely away from the job that put Billy inside and who'd stowed the take for later retrieval, Billy's share included, before turning stoolie and state's evidence and claiming he had no idea where the money'd gone. Billy D wanted him to know he was remembered, wanted to "send a birthday card," as he said when we got together later that day in the mess hall. Fried Spam the color of new skin that grows in after severe burns lay across the top half of our aluminum plate-trays, limp greens in the compartment lower right, watery mashed potatoes beside them.

"Just so he knows who the message is from," Billy told me. "The message itself, the form it takes—that's up to you. You're an imaginative guy, right? Things stay on track, I walk in four, five years. No way Roy's not countin' down. I just want to help him along some, get him to thinking what he has to look forward to?"

"I'll give him your best regards."

Though it had the texture of soggy bread, Billy used knife and fork to cut his Spam into small, precise squares. He'd stoke a bite of Spam into his mouth, follow it with half a forkful of mashed potatoes, then another of greens from which a pale, vaguely green, vaguely greasy liquid dripped onto his denim shirt.

"Roy ain't near as nice as me."

"Then maybe I'll give him more than just your regards."

Billy smiled, showing narrow brown teeth, Spam, and a stalklike strand of greens.

At the next table a con scooped food towards his mouth with two bent fingers. Weighing all of ninety-eight pounds, he was built, nonetheless, like a fat man: head seated directly on shoulders, biceps out from the body, thighs like repelling magnets, knees splayed, feet at a V. Billy watched a moment and shook his head.

"Man don't care for himself, respect himself, how's he expect anyone else to?"

"Wish it were that simple."

"Yeah. Yeah, that poor sorry bastard's every last one of us, ain't he? Like a goddamn fingerprint." Billy's attention shifted. "Look, I appreciate this, Turner. Goes to prove what I've said all along."

"All along, huh?"

He smiled again, Spamlessly this time. "Long enough."

And it was. We'd all washed up on the same shore, had to start from scratch here, build for ourselves whatever lives, whatever unlikely likenesses of civilization, we could. Know how people make shadow figures with their hands on the wall? That's what life inside is like, throwing up hard shadows with hands, mind and heart, pretending they're real.

Finished, Billy placed fork and knife side by side, perfectly aligned, handles an inch apart, in the upper portion of the tray.

"Where you from, anyway, Turner? Some world so far off we need a fuckin' telescope to see it. Old man went off to work every morning wearing Perma-Prest white dress shirts?"

"Matter of fact, most of his life, better than forty years— right up till it closed—he worked at the local sawmill. After that, he didn't do much of anything, including getting up from the kitchen table. Old-timey banjo players had a tuning called sawmill. Because that's where all the players worked, in the sawmills, and so many of them had fingers missing. Sawmill tuning, you could play just about anything with a finger or two."

Billy's eyes met mine. "Like I said, we misjudged you."

"It happens."

"Everyone knew you were a cop. But you sure as hell didn't act like one. First few guys that stepped up to you, and the last, they got put down hard. Then you turned into some kind of college boy. Now what the fuck's *that* about? Who *is* this guy?"

"One of you."

"We finally figured that out. About the same time you did."

"Let's move it," the guard called. "Got others waiting here." We stood on line to hand trays through an opening at one end of the mess. Beyond, new meat—fresh arrivals, who always drew KP—scraped leftovers into fifty-gallon bins, hosed trays down at stainless-steel sinks, and fitted them into open racks holding sixty at a time. Sweat pouring off the workers competed with output from the hoses.

We went out into a kind of cloister, cement walkway and overhang, moving two abreast back towards the block. Billy said, "You were in Nam."

"That was a long time ago. Another world. Another life."

"In here, everything's a long time ago. Everything's another life."

I nodded.

"How many worlds and lives you think we get?"

Out here the yard looked open, patches of grass and weed sprouting off the walkway, walls far enough away that, if you kept your head down, you could almost imagine they weren't there, though never forget they were.

★ ★ ★

THE WORLD'S A TERRIFYING PLACE WHEN you first come back to it. So much motion, so much noise, the whole of it barking and snapping about you, out of control. Just to get by, to cross a street, go for a walk, see a movie, requires dozens upon dozens of choices. Been a long time since you had to make choices, and the world just won't hold still, it keeps fidgeting, keeps demanding choices. Ordering a soft drink can paralyze you.

I took my free bus ride back to Memphis and, state-issue cardboard suitcase with its freight of books and diploma stowed beneath the bed, settled into a motel at city's edge, Paradise Courts, intending to stay only until my business was done but in fact remaining long afterwards, almost two months as it turned out, for lack of what my father doubtless would have called gumption. I was barely able to brave the day's wading pool of choices; no way I could face the sea of what to do next. Those first few days, I made promised contacts, delivered messages and keys, shuttled a package or three between stations, met up with Roy. All of it went smoothly enough that on the fourth day, Tuesday, I found myself emptied of short-term goals, sitting in a bar at eleven in the morning.

The sign out front of Paradise Courts was shaped like a painter's palette, powder-blue sky visible through the thumbhole, letters of the name in a fan of bright colors long since faded. Pure 1950s. The motel itself consisted of two levels of rooms, six on top, eight below, sketchy rail running along the upper tier, stairway at either end. Lower rooms opened directly onto parking lot, skinny moat of shrubs, interstate service road. Whenever anyone went up or down the stairway, walls shook and glasses fell off tables. Buffalo

Nickel Diner, where daily I tested courage and fortitude, sat just past the edge of the motel's mostly unused parking lot; Junie's Bar, a concoction of cinder block and brown-painted wood, just past that.

You never get too far from the smell of the river and magnolia blossoms in Memphis. At Paradise Courts you were never far from the smell of the diner's Dumpsters, or from view of the swarm of derelicts, drunks and other dead-enders forever lurking behind Junie's.

Junie himself was a hunched, long-limbed man in his early sixties whose low brow and darting eyes underlined a monkeylike appearance. He always wore a blue dress shirt with button-down collar, sleeves folded back twice, and jeans. Jeans and shirt alike, including folded sleeves, were ironed; creases had gone white. Afternoons you'd find Junie sitting at the end of the bar reading old copies of *Popular Science* and *Saga* he bought in batches off a friend who had a used-book store. He'd look to the door as you came through, swing off his stool and be waiting behind the bar by the time you reached it. If you were a regular, your usual would be waiting.

I wasn't a regular. I'd been in a few times those past four days, including the night I shut the place down sitting three stools away from the bar's only other patron, a well-dressed woman a decade or so younger than myself. Her simple black dress hung loosely while somehow suggesting what lay beneath. When she lifted her glass, hooplike silver bracelets slid down her wrist and rings caught light. We'd spent the final hour lobbing verbal sallies back and forth, buying one another drinks, careful never to breach the three-stool safety zone.

Junie drew the beer I asked for and handed it across.

"Dollar-ten."

I put two singles on the bar and swung knees from beneath the overhang, north-northeast to south-southwest, to look out across the service road. Skimpy trees bowed in the spillage of wind from the interstate. Clouds crept slow as glaciers across the sky. Downing the beer in a couple of gulps, I asked for another. Junie brought it and stayed on. Eyes strayed to the TV propped up on old telephone books at the end of the bar, where a sexy older woman reminded her lover how passionate they'd once been, how much things had changed, and asked him, again and again, why. Leaving aside production values, you knew this couldn't be anything but a soap opera. Soap operas were the only place on TV where sexy older women happened.

"You're Turner, right? Over at Paradise?"

I admitted to it.

"Surprise you to hear the man's been poking around, asking questions?"

"Not really."

"Local, from the look of them. Already been up and had a check of your room too, would be my guess."

I put another couple of dollars between us. Magically they became a beer. Onscreen a young man with silver crosses for earrings, electric blue eyes and crow-black hair, radiating indolence and ambition in equal parts, spoke intensely into the camera.

"Just back on the street?" Junie asked.

"Coming up on a week."

"And seems a lot longer, I bet. You doing okay?"

"Know that much about it, do you?"

"Some. Most of my life, before I came upon these gracious

165

surroundings you see about you"—his arm dipped and rose, pass of the bullfighter's cape—"I was a cop."

That night I closed the bar down again and then some, sitting not three stools away from Madam Mystery but across from, then beside, the bar's owner. I'd let on that I'd been a cop, too, so for better than an hour we swapped war stories. Then for a time we sat silently.

"Married?"

"Way back."

A coven of sirens screamed by outside. Fire truck, medics, a patrol car or two, from the sound of it. On the interstate, or closer by?

"People wonder why the hell I keep this place open," Junie told me. "Guys I was on the job with come in here, have a beer, look around and shake their heads."

Beers had been filing past as though on parade, each stepping proudly into the former's place. Then everyone else was gone, doors locked, single light still aloft above the bar, jukebox unplugged in favor of bluegrass from a cassette player by the cash register. Junie ferried out to the kitchen to fetch back a pizza. "Frozen," he said, "but I threw on real mushrooms and sausage before it went into the oven." I recalled a pizza I'd had years ago in one of Memphis's very first trendy restaurants, back when Beale Street was just starting to get dug out from under and Mud Island turned into a shrine: squirrel with feta cheese and artichokes. What's next, I'd wondered then—possum with pesto on a bed of grits?

Side by side, men of constant sorrow, Junie and I smacked lips, licked grease and molten cheese from fingers, went after runaway bits of sausage and mushroom.

166

"Time was, we'd get most anyone heading for Ozark retreats, Hot Springs or Nashville through here, plus a hearty tourist trade coming the other way, from Arkansas and Mississippi. They'd eat at local cafés, stay overnight at local motels, buy color postcards, carry home Kodaks of Aunt Sally trying to squeeze through Fat Man's Bluff. Then the interstate went in. Not to mention, not too long after, airlines with cheap fares. All of a sudden we look around and we're a watering hole, a gas stop. Not much reason even to keep the town open, much less the bar."

"But you do."

"Hey, I'd close in a minute, but then what'm I gonna do? Watch shit on TV all day long, get to be a god-awful nuisance to my neighbors, hang out at some senior center learning to drool?"

He brought a couple more beers. The collection was growing. Empty bottles upright on the table like gunnery, obelisks, small monuments.

"Back when I was young," Junie said, "new on the force and married? I'd come home and find my wife just sitting there, looking out the window. Took a long time before I understood. You always wonder, afterwards, how you could ever have been so oblivious. But once I got so I could see the pain in her face, the pain at the center of her, I wasn't able to see much else."

Years to come, I'd spend much of my life sitting alongside other people's pain as I did that night, hearing it break, stammer, circle back on itself, duck, feint and run. I'd remember this moment.

"We'd been married almost four years when she died," Junie said. "I came home one morning and found her in the tub. She was leaning back, eyes closed. The water was cold. So was she. I've had a soft spot for junkies ever since."

He got up to shove in a new tape. Some early western swing group, Milton Brown maybe, doing "Milk Cow Blues." For a time Brown had this amazing steel guitar player, Bob Dunn, a natural on the order of Charlie Christian or Johnny Smith, played steel like it was a jazz trombone. His breaks gave you chills.

I got back to the room around three in the morning and, unable to sleep, lay watching lights from the interstate sweep the wall, radio on low beside me, both of them messages from a larger world beyond. Finally dawn's foot caught in the door. I hauled myself from bed, showered and went out to the diner for breakfast. When I returned, there was a lock over the doorknob of my room. Looked like a big clown's nose.

A young redhead with half a yard or so too little shirt and half a dozen too many tattoos manned the office. He hooked his head as I came in, swiveled the phone up from his mouth and said he'd be with me in a minute.

"Can't get in my room," I said when he finished.

"Two-oh-three, right?"

"Yeah."

"Need you to pay up."

"I've been paying by the day, almost a week now. It's not due till noon."

"We're talking yesterday, not today."

"I brought money by around ten."

"No record of it."

"Short, fat guy, looked like his hair hadn't been washed for, I don't know, maybe ten years?"

"Danny."

I waited.

"Danny's gone. Checked out last night." He didn't think it was funny either, but hey. "With everything in the till, not to mention the office radio."

"And my money."

He shrugged. "Don't guess you have a receipt."

I did, as it happened. In prison you learn to hoard, you hang on to every single thing that comes your way.

Red studied the receipt, did everything but sniff it, and grunted. I paid him for the day. He grunted again.

"Be a lot easier if you paid by the week."

I just looked at him, the yard look, and watched his face go smooth. He pushed a receipt across the desk without meeting my eyes again. Then he got a bunch of keys and followed me up the staircase to unboot the door. The keys were hooked onto a giant steel safety pin and rang like tiny wind chimes as we climbed.

Inside, I switched on the TV to the rerun of an old cop show, some five-foot guy with a chip on his shoulder the size of a river barge and a taste in clothes running to big collars, slick fabrics and rips. All his shirts seemed to be missing the top three buttons. A gold medallion nestled in there among chest hair. I found myself wondering what it would be once it hatched.

Paired footsteps moyed up the stairs.

Someone knocked at the door.

Cops and cons, you always know. Way they stand, way they walk, something in the eyes. The point man was there almost flush with the door, smiling, relaxed, but ready to push in or take me down if he sensed the need. He was one of the rare individuals whom off-the-rack fit perfectly; his dark

JCPenney suit was immaculate, carefully pressed, but slick with wear. His partner (who'd be driving the Crown Vic pulled in at an angle below) stood off by the railing. Seersucker for him, spots baked into the tie.

"Mr. Turner?"

I nodded.

"Mind if we come in?"

I backed off and sat on the bed. Tugging up pantlegs to save the crease, Big Dog took the chair past the nightstand. B-side stayed on his feet just inside the door. He held a hand-carry radio unit. Every few moments it crackled.

"Can't help but notice you didn't ask to see badges. Situation like this, most people would."

"I'm not most people."

"True enough." He looked around, as though the limping dresser or precise angle of the bathroom door might divulge something crucial. "Nice place. Been here what? four, five days? Like it?"

"I've seen worse."

He nodded. B-side lifted the curtain to look out. "Hey! Get away from there!" he hollered. "Fuckin' kids." He stepped out onto the walkway and continued in the same vein, after a moment came back.

"You know a man named Roy Branning, Turner?"

"I could."

"Four-oh-four Commerce Parkway? You paid him a visit two nights ago."

"Carrying a message. Nothing more to it than that."

"And the message was?"

"Private."

"Sure it was." He got up and walked into the bathroom,

came back holding my safety razor. "Private's a word you need to be careful around. You know?" Sitting again, he ran the razor along the edge of the nightstand, digging in. Veneer peeled off, thin shavings curled up behind. "Thing is, day after your visit, Branning turned up dead. We have to wonder what you know about that. Surprise you?"

"Not really. What I hear, he was pretty much the complete asshole."

"You heard right." This from B-side by the door.

"So there's nothing you can tell us? Now, when it could make a difference? Before this all goes any further?"

I shook my head.

He set the razor carefully on edge on the nightstand, stood and ambled towards B-side, who shifted the radio between hands to open the door.

"We'll be in touch."

"Be careful out there, Detective."

"Thank you for your concern. So few care."

His smile put me in mind of a throat cut ear to ear.

# Chapter Twenty-Five

CHICKENS MAY NOT HAVE A LOT on the ball, but once they start, they do go on. Velma's boy looked like what gets tossed off a butcher's block when everything remotely useful's been hacked away.

"Two violent deaths since you showed up here," Lonnie Bates said. "This sort of thing follow you around?"

"Could look that way, I guess." Did to me sometimes.

We stood over the cadaver with Doc Oldham. I was thinking how the words *cave* and *cad* were in there. I was thinking how frail our lives are, how thin the thread tethering us to this world. Go out for the Sunday paper and on the way back, half a block from home, you get hit by a delivery truck. Random viruses claim squatter's rights in our bodies and won't be evicted. Amazing any of us manage to stay alive.

"Lonnie, goddamn it, I got people to take care of. Live people. Not much I can do for this poor son-of-a-bitch, is there?"

"County pays you, Doc."

"Every village's gotta have an idiot." He wore good-quality

clothes, Brooks Brothers tan suit, blue oxford-cloth shirt, carefully cinched tie—all so stained and body-sprung that Salvation Army sorters would have thrown them out. Half a mug of coffee disappeared at a single swallow. The mug had a nude woman on it. When you poured in hot liquid, her flesh disappeared and a skeleton emerged. As the contents cooled, flesh came back. Right now, she was about half formed. "Dozen more bodies, I might even be able to make my car payment this month, who knows?"

"What can you tell me?" Bates asked.

"Chickens ate him."

"Thank God we have you. All those years of study, all that expertise. Without that, where would we be?"

Doc Oldham shrugged. "If I wasn't here, why the hell would I care in the first place? Hell, I don't care now. Velma okay?"

"Don Lee's with her. Niece on the way up from Clarksdale. Only family she has."

"Igor!"

An elderly black man looking like a 1950s railroad porter appeared to claim stretcher and remains of body and wheel them away. Doc Oldham followed. Much-abused stainless steel doors swung to behind.

We walked out into stiffling heat, early-morning rain dripping from trees and eaves and steaming off the sidewalk.

"What's your day look like?" Bates asked.

"Assuming you don't have other plans for me, it looks like a drive into the city."

I'd spoken to Val and got the name of a guy who wrote about movies and taught film studies at the university. His books sported titles like *Biker Chicks and Fifty-Foot Women,*

*Short on Clothes, Skateboard Cowboys.* He'd written an entire book, Val said, on the three versions of *Invasion of the Body Snatchers.* Kind of books Carl Hazelwood might have had out in the garage, from the sound of things. Guy's a little weird, Val added. What a surprise.

Just over two hours later I found myself on a block-long street a mile or so off campus where restaurants, cafés, coffee shops and bars still tilted their hats towards students. St. Martin's Lane didn't exist on any map; I'd had to stop and ask directions three times. Then, when I found the address, there was no house on the lot. Five-fourteen gave way directly to 518, with a spot between like a missing tooth. A structure stood back by the alley fence, though, a guest house or converted garage. I pulled into the ruins of a driveway and headed for that.

What at first glance I took to be a small, hunched man answered my knock. On closer notice I realized he wasn't small at all, only drawn into himself, so that he gave the appearance of such. He'd been wearing headphones that pulled away when, oblivious, he came to the door and, as it were, the end of his rope. He glanced back at them lying inert on the floor a yard or so behind. Two days' growth of beard, hair chronically unruly, scuffed loafers, baggy chinos with frayed cuffs, a black T-shirt. Over this, a many-pocketed hunter's vest.

Two rooms from what I could make out, possibly another beyond? Shutters and curtains drawn. The whole of it seemed to be lit with a single 40-watt bulb.

"You're Turner? Come on in."

He showed me his back as he scuttled into, yes, a third room, and came back with a platter from which he peeled off plastic covering. Carrot sticks curled up like the toenails of old men, cheese cubes awash with sweat. I had the impression my host didn't entertain often and was into recycling.

Having delivered the goods, he bent to retrieve the headphones and put them on a table beside a rickety recliner.

"I was just having a beer," he told me, and picked up a can of Ballantine Ale. Tilting it back only to find it was empty, he looked puzzled, as with the headphones. "Maybe that was earlier, come to think of it. Have one with me?"

"Sure."

Again, back to me like a beetle, he exited. A hairless cat materialized at my feet, throwing itself to the floor in elaborate shoulder rolls. On a TV in one corner a black-and-white movie showed soundlessly. Long, back-projection shots of highway-patrol cars coursing down highways. Arizona? New Mexico?

My unaccustomed host stood in the doorway, beer in each hand. His name was Mel Goldman. He survived off novelizations of B-grade movies and TV series. Half a dozen paperbacks he'd written around a show concerning L.A. teenagers' crises (things are hell out there in the promised land!) did okay in the States but went gold in Germany. Publishers brought him over, major national magazines interviewed him. I almost shit my pants, he'd said of the experience upon return. Those people had to know I'm a Jew, right?

"Aliens have landed," Goldman told me. "The sheriff's kid saw them, but no one believes him. He's a dreamy sort. First reel's amazing—just kind of floats. Creates this whole town, this atmosphere of suspicion and dread. Then it all gets thrown away and the whole thing turns into one long, stupid chase. Kind of thing a man would eat his socks not to have to watch."

I tried hard not to look down at his feet.

He handed me a beer and asked what he could do for me. We sat watching a '52 Dodge with a green plastic screen like the brim of a card dealer's hat above the windshield careen off the road as a tall man, strangely stooped, stepped out before it.

"Something about a murder, you said on the phone. I don't see how I could possibly help you with something like that."

I gave him the abstract: my case and Carl Hazelwood's death in fifty words, dry as a science paper. Like notes you make about clients for your files. "I don't know what I'm looking for," I said. "But I read Carl's journal. Lot of it had to do with old films."

"Science fiction, gangster, prison stories—that sort of thing?"

"How'd you know?"

"What else would it be?" He watched as the tall, stooped man entered a cave hidden among trees. " 'Home. I have no home. Hunted, despised, living like an animal.' "

"Okay."

*"Bride of the Monster."*

Onscreen, inside the cave, the tall, stooped man stood over a body laid out on a steel table.

"One of many he'll inhabit," Goldman said. "The bodies, recently dead, are imperfect and last but a short time. His supply is running out, his mission remains unfulfilled."

*That* had a ring of familiarity about it.

"Actor's name is Sammy Cash. No one knows much of anything about him, who he was. He came out of nowhere, starred in this string of movies—for a year or so there, he seemed to be in every cheap movie made—then he was gone."

"Carl's sister says films were realer than life to her brother, that he loved the bad ones best of all."

"Good man. There really is an inverse engine at work here. The cheaper the films are, the more they tell you what the society's *really* like, as opposed to what it claims for itself. Any particular names come up?"

I pulled out my notebook.

"Herschell Gordon Lewis, Larry Cohen, *Basket Case, Spider Baby, The Incredibly Strange Creatures.*"

"Mr. Hazelwood had good taste. Or bad. Depending." He laughed, and beer came out his nose. He wiped it, beer and whatever else, on his sleeve.

"Any idea who or what BR might be? It comes up on almost every page of his journal. An abbreviation, initials—"

"Just the two letters? No periods after?"

I nodded.

"Carl Hazelwood was murdered, you said?"

"You know something?"

"I might. You see the body?"

"Pictures."

"Like this?" Goldman brought his arms over his head in an acute V, wrists turned outward.

I nodded.

"Certain circles, that's a famous image. Couple of Web sites even have it as part of their logo. Branches breaking off. The leaves look like hands."

"Okay, I'm lost."

"You're supposed to be. Know much about cult films?"

"Nothing." Basic interview skills. Play dumb, admit to nothing. Interviewee's words rush in to fill the void. "Tell me?"

"I can do better than that. Hold on."

He stalked off to the corner of the room, rummaged in a stack of videocassettes there, then went to the desk for similar rifling. Came up with a CD. He ejected the resident cassette just as the tall, stooped man passed into a new body.

"This is all I have," he told me, "all anyone has, as far as I know. Downloaded it from an Austrian Internet site."

Long shots of suburban homes, tailored green lawns, billboards. Then suddenly, jarringly, the close-up of a man in agony. He stands or is propped against what may be a trellis, wooden lacework through which a white wall shows. His arms are pushed into a tight V above his head. There is a flurry of hands, four, then six, then eight, as they circle his, touch them, loop twine about wrists, tie them to the open weave. Left alone now, his hands droop to the sides. He smiles.

My host ejected the cassette as the screen filled with static.

"Sammy Cash again," he said, "though most people don't realize it. He'd been through a lot by then, he'd changed. This clip may be all that's left—all I've ever seen, at any rate. But the film's a legend. Any serious collector would trade his grandmother for a copy, throw in his firstborn."

"Why?"

"You mean besides the fact that no one else has one."

"Right."

"Because it's the most elusive movie ever made. There are still a few people around that claim to have seen it, but just as many insist no such film ever existed—that the whole thing's a legend."

He replaced the former cassette. A nude young woman looked in the mirror and saw there the tall, stooped man she'd previously been. She reached out to touch the mirror but, unaccustomed to her new body, reached too hard. The mirror broke.

"*The Giving.* Interesting enough in itself, from what we know. But infinitely more interesting as the last legendary film of a legendary director. You need another beer?"

I told him I was fine. Sipped from my can to demonstrate.

"The director is almost as elusive. Supposedly started out as a studio salesman, flogging film bookings to small theatres all over the Southwest. In the only interview he ever gave, he said he made the mistake one day of actually watching one of the things he was selling and knew he could do a lot better. He sold his Cadillac, sank the money he got into putting together a movie. Friends and neighbors and his barely covered girlfriend served as actors in that first one. He shot it over a weekend, and when on Monday, driving a borrowed car, he went back out on the road, that was the one he worked hardest to sell.

"Took studio folk a time to cotton to what was going on, even with bookings starting to fall off all through Arizona, New Mexico and Texas. By then he'd put away enough money to make another movie. Four more actually. When studio folk finally caught up with him to fire him, he was coming off the plane from two weeks in Mexico with his girlfriend and actors he'd scrounged from local colleges and had those four new films in the can.

"He was like a lot of natural artists, told the same story over and over. Always a dance between this detective hero and his nemesis. At first the nemesis was nothing more than a cardboard character, a threat, a blank, a cipher. But as time went on, movie to movie, he began to become real. In some of the movies he had extraordinary powers. In others he was seen only as a shadow, or as a presence registered by others. Remember, the director was cranking these out in a week or less. Pouring them directly from his soul onto celluloid, as one critic put it.

"Then, suddenly, they stopped. A year went by. Finally— rumor or legend has it—his swan song: *The Giving*. This great mystery movie. There are half a dozen Web sites devoted to his work."

"Can't help but notice you've avoided the director's name."

"I haven't. No one knows it. The movies were all brought out as 'A BR Film.' No separate director's credit. Just the two letters, no periods after."

I stood, thanking him for his time.

"You want, I could skate around a bit on those Web sites, get e-mails off to my contacts, see what turns up."

"I'd appreciate that."

He tried drinking again from the empty can. "Done, then. I'll be in touch."

I almost stepped on the hairless cat who in lieu of giving up, had decided to outwait me and, when I moved, throw itself bodily in my path. As I tried to regain balance my hand went down hard on the couch. A floorboard near one leg cracked, descending like a ramp into darkness. Such was the unworldly ambience of that place, I wouldn't have been unduly surprised if a line of tiny men with backpacks had come hiking up the tilted floorboard.

"Mr. Turner?"

Yes?

"Sammy Cash, the actor? And whoever it was made the movies? Some think they're the same person."

# Chapter Twenty-Six

ONE OF THE LAST CLIENTS I HAD was a man who had mutilated his eight-month-old son. He'd been two years in the state hospital, where things predictably enough had not gone well for him, and came to me on six years' probation, with weekly counseling sessions mandated by the court. I got calls from his PO every Friday afternoon.

Affable, relaxed and clear-eyed, he was never able to explain why he'd done it. Once or twice as we spoke, without warning he'd fall into a kind of chant: "Thursday, thumb. First finger, Friday. Second, Saturday. Third, Tuesday. Fourth, Friday." He seemed to me then like someone trying to express abstract concepts in a language he barely understood. He seemed, in fact, like another person entirely—not at all the quiet young man in chinos and T-shirt who weekly sat across from me chatting.

That's facile, of course. Though hardly more facile than much else I found myself saying again and again to clients back then in the guise of observation, advice, counsel, supposed compassion. Conversational psychiatry has a shamefully limited vocabulary, pitifully few conjugations.

"I just want to get in touch with my wife, my son," Brian would say. "I just want to tell them ..."

"What do you want to tell them?" I'd finally ask.

"That ..."

"What?"

"... I don't know."

My apartment was across from a charter school. Through the window Brian's eyes tracked young women in plaid skirts, high white socks and Perma-Prest white shirts, young men in blazers, gray trousers, striped ties. Eventually I'd pour coffee, mine black, his with two sugars. We'd sit quietly then, comfortable in one another's company, two citizens of the world sidestepping it for a moment though both of us had important work to get back to, at rest and at leisure on time's front porch.

We'd been meeting for maybe three months, Brian having never missed a session, when one afternoon I got a call from him. Calls like that don't bode well. Generally they mean someone is cracking up, someone's found him- or herself in deep shit, someone needs a stronger crutch or more often a wrecker service. Brian just wanted to know if I'd be interested in taking in a movie, maybe grab some dinner after.

I couldn't think why not—aside from the covenant against therapists consorting with patients, that is.

I've no idea what movie we saw. I've since put in time at the library looking through files of that day's newspapers. None of those listed rings a bell.

Afterwards we passed on to an Italian restaurant. This part I do remember. Sort of family place where older kids waited table, all the younger kids and Mom were back in the kitchen, and Dad might come sidling up to your table any moment with an accordion or his vocal rendition of "Santa Lucia." Tonight, though, the villa was quiet. Baskets of bread, antipasto, soup, pasta, entrées, dessert and coffee arrived. Both of us turning aside repeated offers of wine.

I can't recall what we talked about any more than I remember the movie, but talk we did, before, during and after, more or less nonstop. Well past midnight outside a jazz bar on Beale I put Brian in a cab.

That was Tuesday. When Brian didn't show up for his Thursday session, I tried calling. When his PO checked in on Friday, I told him about the no-show. We sent a patrol around.

The PO called back a couple of hours later. I was home by then, changed into jeans and T-shirt, bottle of merlot recorked and in the fridge, fair portion of it in the deep-bellied glass before me. Hummingbirds jockeyed for position at the feeder out on my balcony.

Apparently Brian had gone directly home that night and hung himself. Was this what he'd intended all along? Responding officers said a Billie Holiday CD played over and over. He'd made a pot of coffee and drunk half of it as he undressed and got things together. Under his cup was a page torn from a stenographer's pad.

*Wonderful evening,* it said. *Thank you.*

Mild weather tomorrow, the radio promised. A beautiful day. High in the sixties, fair to partly cloudy. But when I woke, wind whistled at my windows and rain blew against them, forming new maps of the world as it dripped down.

# Chapter Twenty-Seven

"I'M NOT SURE THAT'S POSSIBLE."

"Of course it is. I just need a bench warrant."

"To intercept the mayor's mail."

"Only to log it. I wouldn't be reading it."

"Judge Heslep's the one you'd have to see, then."

"Fair enough."

"Forget that. Man has a picture of Nixon and Hoover shaking hands in his office, no way he's going to issue the warrant. You consider just asking?"

"Asking?"

The sheriff shook his head, picked up the phone and dialed.

"Henry Lee? You playing hooky today or what? Taxpayers don't pay you to sit 'round watching *Matlock*... Good point, we *don't* pay you, do we? And let me be the first to say you're worth every last damn penny... Good, good... Got a question for you. Any problem with our looking over your mail for, oh, say the last couple months? ... Well, sure, but whatever you still have at hand. Anything like me, most of it's still in a pile somewhere... Good man... See you then.

"Clear your dance card. Five o'clock at the mayor's," Bates said, hanging up, "for cocktails." When had I last heard someone use the word *cocktails*? "He'll have copies of mail, payment records—whatever he's able to pull together. Said you should feel free to bring a friend."

"I assume you're coming with."

"I kind of got the impression he had Val Bjorn in mind."

"Not Sarah Hazelwood?"

"Hey. It's a small town. Sneeze, and someone down the road reaches for Kleenex."

"How's June?" I asked. She hadn't shown up for work.

"She's all right. Told me you know what's going on."

"Good that the two of you talked about it."

"She's out looking for the son of a bitch, Turner. You have any idea how hard it is for me to stay out of this?"

"I do, believe me."

"Our kids, what we want for them... She's a smart girl. She'll work it out. By the way, Henry told me I should tell you you're a pain in the ass. He also says we're glad to have you here."

Framed in the parentheses of cupped hands, a face appeared at the window. One of the hands turned to a wave. That or its mate opened the door, and a short, stocky man clambered in. He wore dark, badly wrinkled slacks, white shirt with open collar, gray windbreaker. Somehow when he removed the canvas golf cap, you expected him to look inside to see if his hair might have gone along. Wasn't on his head anymore..

"They're at it again," he told the sheriff.

"What *they* we talking about this time, Jay?"

"Gypsies. Who else would I be talking about?"

"Well now, as I recall, last time you came by, it was a busload of Mexicans being trucked in to pick crops. Time before that, it was a carload of 'city kids.' "

"Gypsies," the man said.

"They haven't put a curse on you, I hope?"

"A curse? Don't play with me, Lonnie. Ain't no such thing as curses."

"So what are the gypsies up to, then? Stealing?"

"You bet they are."

"Which is what everyone says about them, same way they talk about curses. But the stealing's real?"

"Yep."

"You saw it?"

"Family of 'em came in to buy groceries. Afterwards, things turned up missing."

"What kind of things?"

"Couple of Tonka trucks, a doll."

"Family had children with them?"

"Course they did."

"You ever been known to pocket a thing or two you didn't pay for when you were little, Jay? Kids do that all the time. Hell, *I* did... Tell you what. You bring me a list of what's missing, I'll go talk to them. Bet your goods'll be back on the shelf before the day's over."

"Well ... okay, Lonnie. If you say so."

"I'll swing by and pick up that list on my way, say half an hour?"

"It'll be ready."

"Hard not to miss the excitement of law enforcement, huh, Turner?" the sheriff said once he was gone.

"Oh yeah."

187

"If you don't mind my asking, just what is it you do all day out there by the lake?"

"Not a lot. That's pretty much the idea. Read, put some food on the back of the stove for later, sit on the porch."

"What I hear, you earned it. Peace, I mean. Sorry we dragged you away, into all this."

"Some ways, I am too."

This, I thought—this was part of what I valued here, sitting quietly, no one afraid of silence.

"Just between the two of us," I said after a while, "I'm not sure I was coming into my own out there, not sure I ever would. Maybe all I was doing was fading away."

Bates nodded, then dropped his boots off the desk and stood.

"Let's go see the king," he said.

★ ★ ★

THE KING, WHO WAS ALL OF TWENTY-ONE, wore a gold-colored shirt from the 1970s. Its panels showed great paintings, the Mona Lisa, a Rembrandt, a Monet. His palace was a battered silver Airstream trailer, one of those shaped like a loaf of bread, mounted behind a Ford pickup. Tea came to the table in a clear glass pot—started off clear, anyway. Hadn't been that for some time, from the look of it. Half a dozen children of assorted size and age sat against the wall watching TV.

"We have talked about this," he said. "Drink, drink. There's lamb stew if you're hungry. No? You are sure? Please let the proprietor know the articles will be returned. I will bring the children into town myself this afternoon and see to it that each of them apologizes to him. Some would say it's in their blood, I know that. But they are, after all, only children." He poured from the pot into a cup and drank, as though to prove it safe. "Thank you for coming to me with this."

"Your father and I always got along, Marek. I never knew him to do anything but what was right."

The king looked over at the kids, out the trailer window to where old women sat around a makeshift table chopping vegetables. "Maybe someone will say something like that about me one day."

"What I've seen this past couple of years, I suspect they'll be saying a lot more."

After finishing our tea, the sheriff and I climbed in the Jeep and headed back to town.

"You'll be wanting to pick up a necktie for the mayor's cocktail party," Bates said after a time, adding, once I'd made no response: "Joking, of course. Hell, you could wear a butcher's apron and waders in there and feel right at home."

A mile or so up the road we both stuck out our hands to wave at Ida chugging along in her cream–over–blue '48 Buick.

"Ask you something?"

I nodded.

"It's personal. None of my business, really."

I turned to look at him.

"You keep leaving things, quitting them, moving on."

"I'm not sure I ever had much of a choice."

"What would you have told a patient who said that?"

"That one way or another, we always make our own choices. Point taken." I watched a hawk launch itself off a utility pole and glide out across fields of soybean. "Much as anything, I think, that's why I quit. Couldn't listen to myself saying these really stupid things, repeating what I'd heard, what I'd read, one more time. It was all too pat—I knew that from the first. We're not windup toys, all you have to do is tighten a screw or two, rewind the spring, adjust tension, and we'll work again."

The hawk dove, and came up with what looked to be a small possum in its talons.

"The simple truth is, I *didn't* make those choices. Never chose to crawl around a jungle some place in the world so far away I hadn't even heard of it. Never chose to shoot my partner, or in prison to kill a man against whom I had nothing, a man I hardly even knew. And I sure as hell didn't call up my travel agent to arrange for an eleven-year holiday weekend in the joint."

True to form, Bates stayed silent.

"I never felt at home, never found a place I fit. Like you can use a wrench that slips, a screwdriver that's not quite right. They're close, you get the job done. But it makes things more difficult the next time. Threads are stripped, the screwhead's chewed all to hell."

Bates pulled hard right and bounced us and Jeep alike down a dirt path through trees. Bags of garbage had been dumped indiscriminately at roadside. Wildflowers and thick vines grew out of a forties-vintage pickup as though it were a window box. Bates pulled up at DAVE'S, a boathouse, bait shop and occasional barbeque joint built into a low hill alongside the lake and extending on stilts into it. DAVE'S didn't seem to be doing much business. Or any business at all. A lone truck not looking much better than the one sprouting vines back on the dirt path sat in the parking lot.

Bates climbed down and went inside. He was gone maybe five minutes.

"Everyone's okay. I don't get out this way all that often, always like to check on Dave and the family when I do. Been tough for them and people like them, these last few presidents we've had."

We made our way back onto the main road. A camel ride. Bates popped the top on a Coke, handed it over. I drank and sent it back. A couple of miles passed.

"Folks 'round here appreciate what you do for them?" I asked. "They even know?"

"Some do. Not that that has a lot to do with why I do it."

We were coming into town now. Serious traffic. Two, maybe even three cars at the intersection. We pulled up at city hall. Neither of us moved to climb down from the Jeep.

"Sometimes I think the first choice I ever made, my whole life, was when I packed all the rest of it in and came here."

"Hope it works out."

"Better than in the past, you mean."

"No, I just mean I hope it works out."

★ ★ ★

THE MAYOR'S HOUSEKEEPER, a black woman by the name of Mattie, had been with the family over fifty years.

" 'Cept for the spell I got work up to the packing plant," Mattie said. "Always did like that job."

"Woman changed my diapers."

"Liked that job a *lot.*"

She had glasses shaped like teardrops, permed hair that put me in mind of those flat plastic french curves we used in high-school geometry class.

"Mattie's part of the family," the mayor said. That peculiar,

Faulknerian thing so many southerners espouse. It's always assumed you know what they mean. If you ask questions, they swallow their ears.

Mattie brought in platters of fried chicken and sweet corn dripping with butter, bowls of mashed potatoes, collard greens and sawmill gravy, a plate of fresh biscuits and cornbread. Two pitchers of sweet iced tea.

"You-all need anything else right now, Mister Henry?"

"How could we? Looks wonderful."

"Reckon I'll start in on the kitchen, then."

The mayor set his unfinished bourbon alongside his tea glass. We'd been having drinks on the patio when Mattie called us in to dinner. Mine was a sweet white wine from one of those boxes that fits in the refrigerator and has a nozzle. You milk it like a cow.

Out on the patio the mayor had given me a thick manila envelope.

"Here's everything I could find. Won't claim it's complete."

"Okay if I give you a call once I've had a chance to look through it?"

"Don't know as I'd be able to add much, but sure."

Dinner-table conversation took in the high-school football team, how the mayor's wife was doing, a bevy of local issues ranging from vandalism at the city park and cemetery to the chance of a Wal-Mart, the latest scandal surrounding a longtime state congressman, the status of our investigation.

"Do the initials BR mean anything to you?" I asked.

The mayor, who a moment ago had been arguing passionately that the town *had* to bring in new blood, leaned back in his chair. He'd been to the well for more bourbon and now sat sipping it. Dinner was a ruin, a shambles, on the table before us.

"Should they?"

"I don't know… Maybe I'll take some of that bourbon after all, if you don't mind."

The mayor stood. "Lonnie?"

"Why not?"

He came back with two crystalline glasses maybe a quarter full. He'd replenished his own as well. We strayed back out onto the patio.

"Thing is," I said, "Carl Hazelwood's murder has … what university types would call resonance. The circumstances of his death match those of a movie called *The Giving.*" I held my arms above my head, wrists turned out. "Man dies like that. Like Carl Hazelwood. Don't suppose you've seen it."

"Haven't even heard of it."

"Yeah, it's obscure, all right. What they call a cult movie these days. Actor playing the man who dies, his name was Sammy Cash. No one knows who the director was. Went just by his initials: BR."

I dropped it then. We cruised through another half-hour or so of pleasantries before the sheriff and I took our leave. Mattie waved from the front window.

"So?" Bates said.

"So, what?"

He glanced sideways, grinning.

"Okay, okay. I saw something, picked up on something, when I was talking about the film. I'm just not sure what."

"Mayor's gone out of his way to be of help on this. Not like Henry Lee to be so accommodating."

"What does that mean?"

"Jesus, man, is this what happens when you go to college— just like my parents said? You have to always be asking what everything means? I *said* what I meant."

Bouncing on ruts, we made our way towards the main road ahead. We'd reach it someday. Smooth sailing from there on out.

In the distance four loud cracks sounded.

"God, I hope that's someone setting off fireworks for a holiday I forgot."

His beeper sounded.

"There goes hope."

# Chapter Twenty-Eight

BIG DOG AND B-SIDE TURNED UP again a couple of days later, just after eight in the morning.

"Sure hope we didn't wake you."

"Nope. First thing I do every morning, get the day started right, is sit around without clothes on watching the news. Like to keep up."

"We brought some news about your friend Roy Branning."

"Hardly my friend."

"Hardly anybody's," B-side said.

"Seems he may have been put down by one of his … associates. Nothing to do with you. What do you think?"

"I don't, before noon."

"We got on to this the way we get on to most things. Guy we see regularly, what we call a CI, heard some loose talk in a bar, passed it on. But then, you know about CIs."

We were still standing in the doorway, where my clothes weren't. When a young couple passed on the balcony, the girl did a double take. I felt my penis stiffen.

"Don't draw your weapon unless you're prepared to use

it," B-side said.

Funny stuff.

Big Dog glared at him.

"We know about you, Turner. Word's come down to leave you alone, though. We don't much like that."

"Who would?"

"Right." He stepped back, forcing B-side to scramble out of his way. "Who *would* like that? Or for that matter, who'd give enough of a shit to pay attention to what some desk jockey wants, you know? Anyone wants this job can have it. Hell, I'll gift-wrap it for them, got a nice pink ribbon I've saved." He half-lifted one hand in mock benediction. "Be seeing you, Turner."

I went back to bed and was enjoying a luscious meal at a swank restaurant, accompanied by a woman every bit as luscious and swank, when a knock reached in and hauled me out of the dream.

"You Turner?" the small man asked. Something wrong with his spine, as though at some formative point he'd been gripped at head and hips and twisted. Dark hair grew low on his forehead, only a narrow verge of scaly skin separating it from the hedge of eyebrow. Cotton sweater with sleeves and waist rolled, cheap jeans with huge wide legs. "Something for you."

He handed me an envelope.

"Just out?" I said.

"Three days."

"Want to come in, have a drink?"

"Wouldn't say no." He pulled the door closed behind him. "Name's Hogg."

He kept watching me. After a moment I said, "What?"

"I was waiting for the jokes."

"Fresh out of them. Bottle's by the sink in the bathroom. Help yourself. Ice from the machine out by the landing if you want it."

"Ice. *Know* I'm back in the real world now."

He came out with two plastic glasses of brandy as I was reading the note.

*Damn, man, you say you'll take a message out, you mean it! Guess Roy won't have to be worrying about my getting out no longer. RIP and all that crap. Now I'll have to come out and get right on finding that money. Thanks again for carrying for me. Good man. Good luck.*

*Billy D*

"Not that I mind drinking alone," Hogg said, putting a cup down by me. "Alone. In a crowd. With camels." His eyes looked as though they'd been separated at birth and spent their independent lives searching for one another. I lifted the cup in salute or in thanks and drank.

"Got anything lined up?"

"Sure I do. Ninety percent of it'll fall apart before I even get there, way it usually does."

"How many years you pull?"

"Ten to fifteen on my head, little over four underfoot— this time. Met some punk in a bar, both of us half drunk, heard all about his easy score, next thing I know I'm back on the boards. Damned embarrassing. Here I am, supposed to be a pro."

"How'd you find me?"

"I was told where to come."

"Billy D?"

He nodded and, downing what was left of the brandy, stood.

"You're welcome to stay."

"Thanks. But that'll do me." At the door he paused. "You're the cop, right?"

"I was."

"Couldn't have been easy for you inside."

"It's tough for everyone."

Hogg nodded. "I heard about you. You did okay. You helped a lot of people."

My hubris.

Though never in all the years before or since have I needed the excuse of it to make an absolute mess of things.

# Chapter Twenty-Nine

"GODDAMN IT, SUE, JUST PUT the gun down."

She sat on the porch swing, shotgun cradled like a newborn in her arm.

"Where'd you get that thing anyway?"

"It's mine fair and square, Lonnie, don't you worry. I traded for it."

"Alban's hurt, Sue."

"Well I sure as hell do hope so."

"We need to get him help."

"Maybe his girlfriend could help. Why don't you go find her? She'll be hanging around the church somewhere."

The porch was bare boards, couple of feet off the ground, and ran across the whole front of the cabin. The steps were poured cement. They didn't quite match up with anything— ground or porch. Alban lay slumped against them.

"He's bleeding out, Sue."

"Good."

"Now you know I'm gonna have to come up there, put a stop to this."

She shook her head. Raised her left elbow half a foot or so

to emphasize the shotgun.

"Wonder that thing didn't blow up when you first fired it. Crescent, maybe a Stevens, from the look of it. Hardware-store gun. Damn near as old as this town. No one else has to get hurt here, Sue. *Alban,*" he called out. "You okay?"

Alban raised a hand, let it drop.

"Kids with your folks, Sue?"

She nodded.

"Freda's still bringing home those A's, I bet."

Bates stepped out from the shelter of the Jeep and began moving very slowly, hands held in plain sight, towards her.

"They're good kids, Sue. You don't want to leave them alone."

Noiselessly, Don Lee appeared on the porch behind her.

"We head down this road, take a few more steps along it, that's what it could come to."

Don Lee reached across the back of the swing with what I can only call infinite tenderness and took the gun. She offered no resistance, in fact seemed relieved.

Bates returned to the Jeep and picked up the mike.

"June, you there? Come back."

"Ten-four."

"Need an ambulance out to Alban McWhorter's."

"You have it… What's going on out there?"

"I'll be home directly. Tell you about it then."

Don Lee came towards us with Sue in tow. "Alban looks okay to me. Flesh wounds, mostly. My guess is she turned the barrel away at the last moment."

"I'm sorry, Lonnie," Sue said.

"We all are."

"I love him, you know."

"I know."

"He's gonna be okay?"

"You both are. Doc Oldham'll be in touch. We'll let you know what he has to say."

One hand under her shoulder, other at her head, Don Lee guided Sue into the back seat of the squad. She peered out from within, raccoonish.

"Lonnie, can someone call my parents?"

"I'll go by there myself."

They lived in a white house back towards town. It stood out among its peers: paint applied within the last few years, yard recently mowed, a conspicuous lack of abandoned appliances and cars. The curtains were open and, as I soon witnessed, the door unlocked. We could see inside. Past the back of the couch and two heads, animals gone biped strutted and spoke on the TV screen. When we rang the bell, two smaller heads popped up between the larger, facing our way. A handsome woman came to the door.

"Lonnie! How long's it been?"

"Too long as always, Mildred."

He introduced us. A beautiful smile, one eye (lazy? artificial?) that didn't track. You kept wanting to glance off to see what it was looking at.

"You boys come right on in. Horace, see who's here! What can I get you?"

"Nothing, thank you. Heading home to supper the minute I leave here."

Lonnie shook Horace's hand, then introduced me and it was my turn. Horace was a tall man, topped with a thicket of blond, haylike hair. He listed to the left, as though all his life a strong wind had been blowing from the east. Samplers and decoupage adorned every wall. Delicate figurines sat on shelves.

Mildred turned to the children.

"You know, I almost forgot to tell you, but when I went looking for liver in the freezer this afternoon—I couldn't find it, which you have to know, since we ate hamburgers—I saw someone had sneaked a gallon of ice cream in there. I don't know, but I was wondering if, once you're ready for bed, just maybe, you might be interested in trying some."

"It's Sue," Lonnie said once the kids were gone.

"We know what's been going on, Lonnie. Everyone does." This from Horace.

"She's okay. So is Alban."

Mildred: "God be praised."

"Sue somehow got hold of a shotgun. I don't think she meant to do much but scare him. Probably waited for him to come sneaking in—"

"He'd have talked back."

"Always did have a mouth on him."

"Don Lee thinks she turned the gun away at the last moment."

"As she was firing, you mean?" Horace said.

Bates nodded.

"Wouldn't have thought she had it in her."

Horace and Mildred exchanged glances.

"Alban's fine," Bates said. "He'll be out of the hospital in a day or two. There'll have to be a preliminary hearing, but that won't come to much. Sue should be back home about the same time."

"We want to keep our grandchildren, Lonnie."

"Sorry?"

"We don't want them to go back there."

"We love Sue—"

"—and Alban—"

"—but this has gone on long enough."

"You want to take Freda and Gerry away from their parents? Sure they have problems. Which of us don't? But you have to know how much they love those kids, what they mean to them. Take the kids away, their lives come to nothing."

"You think we *want* to do this? It's for their own good."

"It always is."

Afterwards I followed him out to the Jeep. Full dark now. Off the road to either side, frogs called forlornly. A moon white as blanched bone hung in the sky. It was some time before he spoke.

"I hate this shit," he said, "absolutely hate it. Everyone's right. And everyone loses."

"True enough." A mile or two further up the road I added, "But from what I see, you do good things here. You help people, bring them together, shore up their lives. Everything we think the job's about when we start."

"Then it changes on you?"

"Or you change. You listen to that hundred-and-tenth explanation and realize you just don't care anymore, you don't want to know. Helping people? Improving the community? Hey! you tell yourself, you're just the dog that keeps the cattle from straying."

Lonnie dropped me at the office. Few days back, he'd loaned me an old car he had sitting in the garage; now I figured to head back out to the cabin. I was looking down at the floorboard, thinking about a patient I'd had, Jimmie, who was convinced not only that he was a machine but also that he had less than a year left in his batteries, when someone rapped at the window. Startled, I turned. No one should ever be able to get that close without my knowing.

I tried rolling down the window, but it didn't, so I got out.

"Once again the true gentleman," Val said. "You hungry, by any chance? One of us owes the other one a dinner, I'm fairly sure."

"I had plans."

"Oh."

"Of course, those plans were only to go home and drink half a bottle of a really good cabernet."

"What, and let the other half go to waste?"

"Seems a shame, doesn't it? Want to see where I live?"

"Are you asking me out?"

"In, actually."

"Better than calling me out, I guess."

"I may even be able to scrounge up a handful of rice."

"Not brown, I hope. Never can be sure, with you monkish types." She walked around to the other side. "And I get to ride in this cool car, too! Lucky girl."

Between us, she pulling from without, me pushing from within, we managed to get the door open. Soon we were well out of town, exiled to the moon's province, in the company of owls. Neither of us said anything about how beautiful it was out here, though we both thought it.

"By the way," Val said, "did I mention I've just had the worst day of my life?"

"Not that I recall."

"No? Good. I was hoping I wouldn't bring that up."

The radio functioned on a single station: dim patter and

songs from the twilight of the race. Val twirled the knob, found static, and spun it back. Herman's Hermits, girl groups, "Under the Boardwalk." She settled back, let her head rest, and moments later seemed asleep.

"I'm not," she said when I pulled in at the cabin. "Almost, but not quite. Drifting ..." She turned towards me. Green eyes opened and found mine.

We went inside.

"Whoa, why do I feel I'm walking right into someone's head?"

"Things had gotten way too complicated. I wanted them as simple as they could get."

Old wooden kitchen table by the window, a single chair. Bed across from it—little more than a cot, really. Shirts and pants on hangers hanging from nails in the wall. Stacks of T-shirts, socks and underwear stowed under the cot. Basin and pitcher on the counter. (Pump just outside.) Toothbrush and razor laid out there. Books in undisturbed stacks along the back wall.

I popped the cork on the wine, one of those new plastic ones, and suggested we sit on the porch.

"Maybe I should hold out for jelly glasses."

"And potted meat on toast points."

The low, indefinable susurrus that's a part of living in the woods sounded around us. Always that or dead silence, it seemed. Far off, something screamed once, a spear thrown into the night. We watched a silhouette, possibly two somethings, cross the moon.

"The world's a shithole, isn't it?"

I reached for the bottle on the floor by my chair and freshened our drinks. An Australian wine, 1.5 liters. We would run out of conversation before we ran out of wine. Picture of a koala on the label, an endangered species. As though we all aren't.

"Except for music," she added.

Then, after a moment: "I don't know if it's myself or the job anymore. Seems whatever door I open, I don't like what's in there."

She held out her glass for more wine.

"You remember that night we sat out on my porch, hardly talking, with the night so quiet around us?"

I nodded.

"I think about that a lot," she said.

# Chapter Thirty

NOT MANY SHIFTS GO THAT WAY. Most of them, you hit the street already behind, dance cards filling faster than you're able to keep track of. We spent the biggest part of that one rattling doors and doing slow drags down alleys. Had no calls for better than two hours, and when we finally got one it was a see-the-lady that turned out to be about a missing husband. We were twenty minutes into the call and halfway done taking a report when her response to a routine question stopped me in my tracks, follow-up questions eliciting the information that the man had died ten years ago.

Back in the squad, I sat shaking my head.

"What?" Randy asked.

"That one."

Randy glanced over as I pulled away from the curb.

"You notice the open kitchen window?" he said. "Saucer of milk on the sill?"

I admitted I hadn't.

"Woman's lonely, that's all. So lonely that everything in her life takes on the shape of her loneliness."

The next call was to a convenience store where the owner-proprietor supposedly had a shoplifter in custody. He'd taken a jump rope off one of the shelves and tied the shoplifter to it after a baseball bat to the thigh brought him down. But while he was on the phone, the shoplifter had chewed through the rope and gone hobbling out the door.

Nothing else, then, for some time. It was one of those clear, still nights that seem to have twice as many stars as ordinary, when sounds reach you from far away. We grabbed burgers at Lucky Jim's and ate at a picnic table outside East High, squad pulled up alongside with doors open, radio crackling. You didn't eat Lucky Jim burgers in the car. And you didn't need extra napkins, you needed bath towels.

Randy seemed to be doing okay. He'd moved out of the house, put it up for sale, found an apartment near downtown. He was hitting the gym at least three times a week, even talked about signing up for some classes. In what? I asked. Whatever fits with my work schedule, he said.

Three obviously stoned college-age kids were having their own meal, consisting mainly of bags of candy, potato chips, orange soda and Dr Pepper, nearby. They packed up and left not long after we arrived. Two people just as obviously on the street sat beneath a maple tree. The man wore a Confederate cap from which a bandanna depended, draping the back of his neck and bringing to mind all those movies about the Foreign Legion I watched in my youth. The woman had gone on trying gamely to look as good as possible. She'd hacked sleeves from a T-shirt whose logo and silkscreen photo had long since faded and cut it off just above the waistline. Rolled pant legs showed shapely if long- and much-abused calves. "You know that bugs me!" the man shouted towards the end of our stay. She sprang to her feet and started away. "Why you wanna be doing that?" he said, then after a moment got up and followed.

Though we were talking and continued to do so, Randy turned to watch the man go, I remember, and in that moment of inattention a compound of grease, grilled onion and mustard fell onto his uniform top, just south-southwest of his badge. We kept bottles of club soda in the squad for such situations, just as we kept half-gallons of Coke, useful for cleaning battery terminals and removing blood from accident scenes. But in this case the club soda lost, serving only to create concentric rings around the original stain.

We pulled out of the lot. Traffic was light.

"You give much thought to what we'll be when we grow up?" Randy said. "I mean, here we are, top detectives, still jumping patrol calls. That sound like a life to you?"

"We like patrol calls. It's our choice."

"Is it?"

When the radio sounded ten minutes later, we looked at one another and laughed. Randy was asking if I'd consider accompanying him to temple that Sabbath.

"You've been going to temple? When did that start?"

"You know when it started."

"And it's okay for me to be there?"

We pulled up at 102-A Birch Street, a duplex in a recently fashionable part of town. Property values had rocketed here. Years later they'd coin a word for what was going on: gentrification. Bulldozers plowed the ground from first light to last, crunching homes, garage-size commercial shops and early strip malls underfoot, making way for new crops.

"You okay?" I remember asking Randy. He'd made no move to get out of the squad.

"Fine," he said. "Just not sure I can do this."

"Do what?"

"Never mind." He swung legs out and stood, with a two-handed maneuver I'd gotten to know well, smoothed down hair and put on his hat in a single sweep. "Forget I said anything."

Wary and watchful as always, we went up the walk to the front door. Several adjacent houses, though well cared for, seemed unoccupied, as did the other half of the duplex. Drapes behind a picture window at the house next door moved. Probably the person who'd called in, monitoring his or her tax dollars at work.

"Mind taking point on this one?" Randy said.

"Nottingham, huh?"

Police superstition. Back sometime in the 1950s, a squad answering a routine call according to procedure had eased up the walk just like us and knocked, only to be answered by a shotgun blast through the front door. The point man, Nottingham, went down, and died in the hospital six days later. His partner, a rookie, did all the right things. Checked pulse and respiration, went off to call in an Officer Down, came back to pack his partner's wounds. Then he kicked in the door and took the perp down with his nightstick. After that, though, after that one perfect moment when he became, incarnate, what he was *supposed* to be, when the training flowed through him like a living force, the rookie was never again able to take to the streets. He tried once or twice, they said; then worked a few years more, filing, keeping track of office supplies, manning the evidence room, before he packed it in.

"I've got your back," Randy said.

"Not my back I'm worried about."

The door was answered by a half-dressed man whose eyes raked over uniform, badge, side arm and equipment belt before settling on my face. Then a secondary, dismissive glance at Randy behind me. From deep inside the house, echoing as in a cave, the sound of a TV. Something else as well?

"Sorry to bother you, sir," I said, "but we've had a report of a domestic disturbance at this address." Going on for hours, the caller said. "Mind if we come in?"

"Well ..."

"I'm sure there's nothing to it. Do have to ask a few routine questions, though. Won't take more than three, four minutes of your time, I promise."

He rubbed his face. "I was asleep."

"Yes, sir. Most people are, this time of night. We understand that."

He backed out of the doorway. I followed into the room. Randy stayed just inside the door. He had yet to speak.

"Someone called, you said?"

"Yes, sir."

"Jeez, I'm sorry. Must have been the TV. My wife has trouble sleeping."

"Yeah, that's probably it."

"Your wife?" Randy said.

"Could we speak to her?" I asked.

"She just got to sleep, Officer. Sure would hate to have to wake her now."

"Please." This time I didn't smile.

He led us down three broad steps from the entryway, across a tiled living room the size of a skating rink, and along a

211

narrow hallway into a small room adjoining the kitchen. Wood-paneled walls, single window set high, cotton rugs scattered about on a floor of bare concrete. Not much here but a couple of chairs and a console TV. A conical green TV lamp sat atop the console—these had just started showing up. The vacant chair was a recliner. The occupied one was an overstuffed armchair, ambiguously greenish brown, and nubbly, like period bedspreads.

The woman in that chair, wrapped in a tiger-pattern throw, makes no response when I speak to her.

"She's not well," the man says. "She's … disturbed. Look at her now. An hour ago she was screaming and beating at me. Walking through the house slamming doors."

"So it wasn't the TV after all."

He shook his head.

"Sounds like you need to get her some help, sir."

"She has plenty of help. I'm the one who doesn't." His eyes go from his wife to me. "Mostly she's up at the state hospital, has been for years now. Home on a pass."

Randy comes around me, sinking to one knee. Presses two fingers against the woman's carotid. "Honey, you okay?" he says, but it doesn't register with me at the time what he's saying.

And afterwards it takes me a long time to understand what happened here.

The half-dressed guy steps forward, out of the shadow. His hand comes up. Something in it? Randy thinks so. He draws his side arm, stands, shouts at the man to drop the weapon and get down on the floor, hands behind his head. What the man has in his hand is a syringe. The woman's diabetic, we learn later. He walks towards her.

Glancing at Randy, shouting *No!* I see what is about to happen and I don't think about it, I react, just as trained.

"What—" Randy says, as I draw and fire. I intend only to stop him, take out the shoulder or arm, but you're taught to go for the trunk, the larger target, and I'm not in the driver's seat this time out, I'm on auto.

Randy goes down.

At first he's conscious, though rapidly heading into shock. I kick the S&W away from his hand, kneel beside him to check pulse and respiration. I'm sorry, I tell him. I go back out to the squad and call in an Officer Down, request a second response unit for the woman. When I get inside again, something's happened, something's gone even more wrong. Blood is pooling all around Randy and his breath comes in jagged bursts, like rags torn from a sheet. I slip out of my sportcoat, take off my shirt and fold it into a compress, hold it against the wound. Almost at once the shirt is saturated with blood. I push harder, hold on harder. My arms quiver and begin to cramp. The shirt darkens. His breathing quietens. Lots less blood now. I tell him again that I'm sorry.

Two or three minutes before the paramedics arrive, Randy dies.

As I said, it took me a long time to understand what had happened here. Turned out Randy knew the place. That's why he reacted the way he did when we first pulled up curbside. Doreen had worked with the guy who lived here, stayed with him for a while after she left Randy, had a brief affair. She'd long since moved on, but Randy was never convinced of that. All these months when I'd been thinking he was getting past Doreen, getting his life back together, he'd been spending much of his off time parked down the street.

The woman in the chair wasn't Doreen, of course. But she looked a lot like her. And to Randy's overloaded mind in that moment of crisis, I guess, in those final moments of his life, somehow she became Doreen. Lying there, looking up, it wasn't me but Doreen that he saw. He lifted a hand as though to caress her face. Then the hand fell.

I saw her, the actual Doreen, looking not much better than I felt, five days later at the funeral. She wore a blue dress. Bracelets jangled as she raised her arm to brush hair back from her face. We told each other how sorry we were, how much we missed him. We said we should keep in touch.

For her it was a promise. Twice a week in prison I'd receive chatty letters from her. They were penned in violet ink on four-by-six-inch lavender pages folded in half and filled with news of new neighbors, newborn children, new stores and malls. She persisted in this for almost a year, heroically, before giving up.

# Chapter Thirty-One

THE OFFICE WAS EMPTY, THOUGH unlocked. Remembering all those hollow, echoing buildings and streets in *On the Beach*, which I'd seen at the impressionable age of fourteen (after which I'd read everything of Nevil Shute's the local library had), I found Lonnie and Don Lee at the diner.

"Out to lunch, huh? Maybe you should just move the sign over here. Sheriff's Office. Hang it up by the daily specials."

"More like breakfast for you, way it looks," Don Lee said. "Just get up?"

"Yeah. Nightlife around here's a killer."

"You get used to the pace."

Thelma materialized beside the booth. "What'll it be?"

I asked for coffee.

"You people come in at the same time, sure would make my life easier." She shrugged. "Lot you care." She slapped a check down by me. "And why the hell should you, for that matter? Rest of you want anything? Or you gonna wait, so's I have to make three trips instead of one?"

"We're fine," Lonnie said.

"For now."

Thelma walked off shaking her head.

"You're both on duty? Where's June?"

"We are," Don Lee said.

"And June's on her way down to Tupelo, best we know." Lonnie glanced out the window, voice like his gaze directed over my shoulder. "Looks like that's where he went once he cut out of here."

"Shit."

"Pretty much the way we feel about it, too," Don Lee said.

Thelma set a cup of coffee by the ticket she'd slapped down moments before. When I thanked her, she might as well have been stuck by a pin.

"I know I have to leave her alone, let her work this out on her own," Lonnie said. "We talked about that. Best I could do is make it worse."

Right.

"You get your message?"

I hadn't.

"Val Bjorn. Says for you to call her."

"Results of the forensics must be in."

"Probably not that. We got those late yesterday."

"And?"

"Not much there."

"There's a copy for you at the office."

I drank my coffee, called Val only to learn from her assistant Jamie (male? female? impossible to say) that she was in court. She bounced my call back around six P.M.

"Hungry?" Val said.

"I could be."

"Think you can find your way to my house?"

"I'll strap on bow and arrow now. Call for a mule."

"Thank God it's not prom night or they'd all be taken."

"Mostly surfing the Internet," I told her not long after, leaning against the kitchen table, nursing a glass of white wine so dry I might as well have bitten into a persimmon. She'd asked how I spent my afternoon. "You wouldn't believe how many Web sites are devoted to movies. Horror films, noir, science fiction. Someone made a movie about garbagemen who are really aliens and live off eating what they collect, which they consider a delicacy. There's a whole Web site about it."

Val tossed ears of corn into boiling water.

"This isn't cooking, mind you," she said.

"Okay."

"I'm not cooking for you."

"Your intentions are pure."

"I didn't cook the salad either."

"Wow. Tough crowd."

"You think I'm a crowd?"

"Aren't we all?"

"I guess."

"How'd court go?"

"Like a glacier." She bent to lower the flame under the corn and cover the pot. "I'm representing a sixteen-year-old boy who's petitioning the court for emancipation. He's Mormon—parents are, anyway. The defense attorney has put every single member of his family and the local Mormon community, all two dozen of them, on the stand so far. And the judge goes on allowing it, in the face of all my objections of irrelevance. Courthouse looks like a bus stand."

"They love him."

"Damn right they do. You know anything at all about LDS,

you know how important family is to them. They don't want to lose the boy—personally *or* spiritually."

"He has some way to support himself?"

"An Internet mail-order business he created. All Your Spiritual Needs—everything from menorahs to Islam prayer rugs. Netted a quarter million last year."

"Has different ideas, obviously."

"He's not a believer. Even in capitalism, as far as I can tell. It's all about pragmatism, I think. He wanted a way out, independence, and that looked good for it. Much of the profit from the company goes back to the very family he's trying to escape."

"Interesting contradiction."

"Is it? Contradictions imply we've embraced some overarching generality. They're the ash left over once those generalities burn down. Particular, individual lives are another thing entirely."

She was right, of course.

"He have much chance of getting the emancipation?"

Val shrugged. "I don't seem to have much idea how *anything's* going to go these days. This dinner, for instance."

"The one you're not cooking."

"Right."

Later, having smeared ears of corn with butter, salt and pepper and chins unintentionally with same, having stoked away, as well, quantities of iceberg lettuce, radish, fresh tomato and red onion dribbled upon by vinegar and olive oil, we sat on Val's porch in darkness relieved only by the wickerwork of light falling through trees from a high, pale moon.

"Back when you were on the streets, you thought you were doing good, right?"

"Sure I did."

"And as a therapist?"

I nodded.

"Still believe that?"

"Yes."

"But you stopped."

"I did. But not because of some existential crisis."

Sitting in the pecan tree, an owl lifted head off shoulders to rotate it a hundred and eighty degrees. Country musician Gid Tanner, with whom Riley Puckett played, was supposed to have been able to do that.

"When I was sixteen, my dad took me to buy my first car. We found a '48 Buick we both liked. Some awful purplish color, as I remember, and they'd put in plastic seats like something from a diner. Car itself was in pretty good shape. But the fenders were banged all to hell, you could see where they'd been hammered back out from underneath, more than once. I was looking for something bright and shiny, naturally, and those fenders bothered me. My father'd been a bit more thoroughgoing, actually checked out the engine and frame. 'It's a good car, J. C.,' he said. 'Just old—like me. Fenders are the first to go.'

"Later that's how I came to see people. The parts that are out there, between you and the world as you move into it, those parts sustain the most damage. Fenders wear out. Doesn't mean there's anything wrong, intrinsically, with the car. The engine may still be perfectly good—even the body."

"Tell me we're not out of wine."

I handed my glass across. Good half-inch left in there.

"We are, aren't we?" She finished it off, set the glass beside her own. "All day long I sat there looking at Aaron. Fans thwacking overhead. Was I helping him—or only further complicating a life that was complicated enough already?"

"You still want to fix things."

"Yes," she said. "I guess I do."

"You can't."

"I guess I know that, too."

"Ever tell you I was once half a step away from being an English professor?"

"One of your earlier nine lives, I take it."

"Exactly. I loved Chaucer, Old English, Elizabethan drama. Read them the way other people watch soap operas and sitcoms, or eat popcorn. Christopher Fry was a favorite.

*"I expect they would tell us the soul can be as lost,*
*For loving-kindness as anything else.*
*Well, well, we must scramble for grace as best we can."*

"That's what we're doing? Scrambling for grace?"

"For footholds, anyway. Definitely scrambling."

"And what does grace look like?"

"Hell if I know."

# Chapter Thirty-Two

BUT I SUSPECTED IT LOOKED MUCH like my face the morning I decided on exemption.

A sleepless night had filled with the gas of random, skittering thoughts and old memories. Around two A.M. I'd watched *The Incredible Shrinking Man* on TV. Went back to bed afterwards, tossed and turned to the accompaniment of Sibelius's First Symphony on the radio and the giant spider that chased me across roof- and tabletops and through a maze of high-school lockers, was up again at five with a cup of cooling, neglected coffee cradled like a Jacob's ladder in my hands, watching long-haul trucks take on cargo across the street. Soon they'd strike out for the new world.

Brian's last message *(Wonderful evening, thank you)* shimmered in my mind. Jimmie the Machine had been found lying on a bench in the park, eyes staring upward into bright sun, pigeons pecking at bare toes. No discernible cause of death revealed by autopsy. That very day a new patient told me how he'd killed a teacher he disliked. What I saw before me was a defeated fifty-year-old man with tonsure, strands of hair clinging limpetlike to his skull, tattoos like a carpet pattern long since faded. What I heard was a teenager who'd never got over being shut out.

Complex creatures fueled by knowledge, understanding and passion—that's how we like to see ourselves. Meanwhile, psychiatry insists we're little more than machines of a sort, broken toys to be mended. Some simple spring or swivel in the mind fails to work right, we jam, give up, misfire. Ask any child advocate. Nine times out of ten, the kid's been abused. Nothing recondite about it. Most of the rest is just smoke and mirrors.

Speaking of mirrors, that morning, looking into one, I saw something I'd not seen before. It didn't last, but for the moment it was there, I recognized it for what it was. Grace, of a sort. Wherever it was I had been heading all these years, I'd arrived. I had simply to off-load cargo now.

The divestment took most of a month. Clients, I passed along selectively to students from my seminars at Memphis State. These were working therapists, many with far more professional experience, if not more personal, than myself. Licensure requires continuing education credits. Bulwarked by such courses as Statistics for Health Care Providers and Personifications of the Other in Interpersonal Relationships, my own had long proved a popular choice.

Practical affairs—the apartment lease, notification of clients and service providers, packing—presented little difficulty. I possessed, still, the inmate's habit of simplicity; had few ties and little of a material sort that couldn't be tucked under wing and taken along or freely abandoned.

That left Susan.

I had had my mind set against any relationship. Bad for me, worse for whoever sat at the other end of the teeter-totter, probably wouldn't do much good for the world at large. Likely to bring on biblical floods, eras of ice, swarms of locusts, for all I knew. Yet there I was, in a relationship, albeit a halting, tentative one. Coming off a horrendous fifteen-year marriage she'd barely survived psychologically, not to mention physically, Susan trod the eggshell court as lightly as did I.

"This prosciutto's amazing," Susan said.

Our favorite restaurant, just around the corner from her studio apartment, restaurant and apartment much of a size. Waitress a six-footer in miniskirt, tube top and platform sandals stumbling from table to table, dark lines drawn about eyes and mouth as though to hold them in place. Hard to imagine her anywhere else. Where in the larger world could this vision possibly fit?

Susan tucked into the restaurant's signature appetizer of melon and prosciutto as I nursed a second espresso. Entrees of pasta with sausage and sauteed spinach, pasta with salmon and asparagus, were forthcoming. We'd brought our own wine.

"You're making another of your sudden turns, aren't you?"

I hadn't even to tell her. She knew.

"I suppose I am."

"That's okay."

Outside, rain broke, sweeping across the parking lot, left to right, like the edge of a hand brushing debris from a tabletop.

"I half expected it, you know," she said. "More than half, at first. But I still had hopes."

Remember the limbo? One dances beneath a pole set lower and lower. That's hope. Only every year the pole goes further up, not down.

"You'll still have them. I'm not taking those with me."

Brought to our table by the owner of the restaurant himself, our entrees arrived. Susan sat quietly as these were put before us, waited as another swing to kitchen and back cast a basket of bread on the shore.

"Yes," she said then. "You are."

# Chapter Thirty-Three

"WE'RE HEADING HOME," Sarah Hazelwood said. "I need to get back to my job while I still have one. Dad's okay here, but he does best with people he knows, familiar surroundings. Doc Oldham says there's no problem having Carl's body shipped home. I wanted to stop by and thank you for all you've done."

Through the window I could see her father propped up in the van's back seat. The sliding door was open, and Adrienne, willowy, protecting, ranged alongside. Something of both shade tree and sentinel in the way she stood there.

"I'm sorry we haven't been able to clear this up."

"You will. And when you do, you can reach me here." Handing over a sheet of paper with multiple addresses, phone and fax numbers.

I'd been saying I'm sorry a lot of late.

"Why?" Susan had responded that night at Giuseppe's. "You've nothing to be sorry for. I made the choices that brought me here."

"You're not responsible for Jimmie's death, or for Brian's," a therapist I'd briefly engaged back in Memphis told me. "You know that as well as I do. So why are you apologizing? More to the point, why are you here?"

"*Then's* ancient history," Lonnie said. "Might as well be the Peloponnesian Wars, Penelope's suitors. Sure they're important, sure they matter. Meanwhile your coffee's getting cold and the warm-blooded person you're supposed to be having dinner with is waiting for you."

Meanwhile, as well, two videocassettes had arrived via FedEx from a specialty store in California. I'd been alerted to their presence by a phone call from Mel Goldman. One purported to be a rough cut of *The Giving*, the other a weird documentary sort of thing put together by some precocious high-school kid in the Midwest, incorporating clips from BR's films and Sammy Cash's appearances elsewhere. The latter was heavy on science fiction, gangster and prison films, including episodes from a fourteen-part serial about a blind man who, "to bring the slate to balance," had been given supernatural powers by "the Queen of Morning." Since I didn't have credit cards, Lonnie let me use his to order copies. The vendor tacked on a healthy fee for express delivery.

I had to borrow a TV and VCR too, from Val this time, but once I had them, those tapes ran continuously. I'd wander out to the kitchen to make a sandwich or brew coffee, return in time to see the blind man lift his cane to halt a school bus as it skewed towards a cliff; step out onto the porch for air and back through the screen door to images of gigantic Sammy Cash, victim of an atomic blast, on a picnic with minuscule nurse-girlfriend Carla; take a brief turn through the woods and come back to that strange beginning of *The Giving*.

It's the crucifixion, the killing, everyone talks about, and the image is a strong one—even if it makes little sense in light of the rest of the movie. In fact, that salutary scene appears to have been added at the last moment. Perhaps when funds were exhausted? When the movie had to be brought to some kind of end, at any rate. By contrast, the early part of the film fairly drips with atmosphere, connection, portent. A man walks down the streets of a city. To either side, almost off camera, we glimpse what life is like for most of those who live here. Dark-eyed, ragged children stand in alley shadows waiting. Women in doorways open blouses to exhibit wilted breasts. Sleepers, or perhaps they are only bodies, lie alongside buildings and in ditches running with excrement. Dogs drink from the ditches and eat from the bodies. Carrion birds wheel above, waiting their turn.

The man sees or registers little of any of this. For him it's daily life. He has purpose, a destination, sweeps through it all. Farther along he passes the window of an apartment behind whose bars a couple sits having afternoon tea and watching TV. The sound track, which to this point has consisted solely of footsteps, growls and horrible slurpings, now echoes the TV inside.

*In breaking news, the territory's governor vows to pursue reelection from his prison cell. "I did nothing wrong," he declaimed in today's press conference, shortly before asking reporters for cigarettes...*

*... On the international front, fifty thousand ground troops were put ashore on Ayatollah Beach around noon today. The invasion force, which was supposed to have struck at dawn, had been given inaccurate coordinates.*

The man is, as it turns out, a detective. He goes into a bar.

"What can I do for you, friend?" the guy behind the bar says. Hair missing from his head is made up for by that growing out of nose and ears.

"Scotch. Whatever's cheap."

The barkeep pours. "Then you've come to the right place. It's all cheap."

Friend grabs hold of the barkeep's wrist.

"Hey, no problem. I can leave the bottle."

"Ice Lady been in today?"

"Who?"

"Cowboy?"

There's a long hold, these two guys with eyes locked as the world, such as it's become, goes on behind and beyond. A young woman in jeans and T-shirt hacked off well above the navel dances alone. Sharp points of her breasts come into focus and the barkeep pours a new Scotch just as we cut to another, seemingly unrelated scene. Then another.

Did these disparate, disjunctive scenes comprise a movie, comprise even the bare outline of one? Were the abrupt cuts and sudden changes (as though the film had constantly to reinvent itself) in fact part of some inchoate aesthetic weave, ultimately unrealized—or simply what happened when some kid in Iowa fancifully patched together snippets and snatches of film?

Finally, the rough cut of *The Giving* and the documentary were birds of a feather. Neither made much sense narratively, both failed to provide much by way of vertical motion while attempting to camouflage this with horizontal busyness. They were jottings, notes, scrapbooks, diary entries, letters to the editor, casual conversation, junk sculpture.

Two things about them stuck, though.

In the documentary, from internal evidence of the films, much was made of twin theses that BR had to be a southerner, and that the films were in fact collaborations between the director and Sammy Cash.

Then the other.

I came back from the kitchen with new ice in a glass of freshly poured, very old Scotch. I'd started the cassette of *The Giving* again before I left; as I reentered the room, credits were running. Ordinarily I'd have paid no attention. Until the movie began in earnest, I wasn't really watching. But a glance brought me up short with the glass halfway to my face, staring at the screen.

Listed as producer was H. L. "Bubba" Sims.

# Chapter Thirty-Four

"IT WAS MAYBE NINE YEARS back, driest season we'd had in a long time. You could sit out on the porch listening to limbs crack and fall, shingles on roofs curl in the heat. Fires had started up in the woods just east and started moving in. Oaks, elms, pines, they all went up like flares. Thought sure we were gonna have to evacuate the town.

"There was this kid over to the funeral home had been there seventy, eighty years, everyone'd taken to calling him Mojo. He'd fallen, jumped or got pushed from a train. Presented with a bill for 108, the family said, 'You all can keep him.' So he got kept, mummified, coffin leaning up in the corner of the back room. Funeral home was sold, Mojo went with it. Poker players'd drag him out each week for luck, prop him up by the table.

"But when it looked like the town was going under, they decided Mojo had to be given a proper burial. Been waiting since 1920, mind you. But they dragged him out, found a clear spot and put him under.

"The fire was maybe four miles outside town when the rains started up. They went on for a week or more. Everything

230

was sodden. Afterwards they never could find where they'd put Mojo in the ground. Old Man Lanningham claimed he hadn't won a hand of poker since."

Lonnie grinned at me across the top of his coffee mug.

"Don't know why I'm remembering that now."

June called the night before, he'd told me. She was on her way home. That son of a bitch was history.

"So, what do we do about this?" Lonnie said.

"I was thinking the best thing'd be to go out to the house."

"Without calling ahead."

"Yes."

"Henry Lee won't much like that."

I shrugged.

"Here I thought no one could keep secrets in a town this size, and Henry Lee turns out to be a Hollywood wheel."

"A small one. Something on the order of a training wheel—if I'm right."

Lonnie levered the mug onto his desk and stood in a single motion, fishing out keys.

"No sense putting it off, then."

Mayor Sims answered the door in a bathrobe.

"Like to get an early start, do you, Henry Lee?"

"Why don't you give it a rest, Lonnie? Better yet, why don't you go do something worthwhile, like shining those damn boots of yours."

"Think they need it?"

"What I think they need is throwing out. Don't suppose you even had the decency to stop and get coffee on the way?"

"Sorry."

Sims ran a hand through thinning hair. "I was at the nursing home all night. Dorothy's taken a turn for the worse.

Started having trouble breathing around ten o'clock."

"Sorry to hear that. She okay?"

"Stable—for the time being, anyway. She's on a breathing machine. Just for a day or two, they tell me, just to give her some temporary support. Doctor taking care of her looks to be about fourteen. Has a diamond stud in one ear, probably comes to work on a skateboard."

"Anything I can do?"

"Not very damn much, aside from telling me why the hell you're out here this time of day."

I don't figure Lonnie'd ever played tennis in his life, let alone doubles, but his instincts were good, and he fell back. This lob was mine.

"I asked you before if you'd come across a filmmaker known as BR."

"And I told you I hadn't."

"Even though you're listed as producer of his last film."

Mayor Sims sat gazing out the window. At porch's edge, by a red-and-yellow feeder looking like some child's crayoned notion of a flower, three hummingbirds did their version of a Mexican standoff.

"There aren't any copies of that movie," he said.

Should he have added: I saw to that? I didn't ask.

"There's a rough cut someone managed to patch together. It doesn't make much sense."

"Believe me, it never did."

Lonnie spoke up. "We need to know what's going on, Henry Lee. What this is all about."

"I understand."

We sat silently as the hummers outside the window went on squabbling. Ferocious little beasts. Fearless. To the east, above a stand of maples, pillowy white clouds, cumulonimbus, began gathering.

"You two feel up for a longish ride?"

"Whatever it takes," Lonnie said.

"Give me a minute. I need to call in to the nursing home, see about Dorothy. Then I'll grab some clothes and we can be on our way."

★ ★ ★

JUST SHORT OF TWO HOURS LATER, having traversed a patchwork of narrow-lane roads through thick stands of oak and evergreen, kudzu and honeysuckle at roadside everywhere, we reached our destination. Mayor Sims and Lonnie sat in front speaking of inconsequential things, how new kids were doing on the football team, rumors of a Kmart, shorter hours at the city dump. Hardly cabbages and kings. Either because he didn't care or from some design to look like trendy folk he saw on TV, Sims wore a sport coat over black T-shirt. I sat on the cramped, shelflike back seat. The radio was on low, a call-in show of some sort. Responding to an impassioned statement on world poverty, today's authority explained that the problem lay in those societies failing to "incentivize" people to go out and "live creatively." Listening to Authority's voice, I mused again that it's not so much accent as rhythm that gives us away. Where stresses fall, the momentum towards sentence's end, pauses on nouns or verbs.

"Take this next right," Sims said. We'd come onto an oasislike eruption of buildings. Service station, feed store, garage. All of them seemed to be still up and running.

Maggie's Café, despite promises of $1.98 breakfasts and daily $2.95 specials painted on the windows, didn't.

"Now left." Bearing us into an unsuspected town.

The first house, built to quarter-scale on antebellum models and set back from the road, was now a real estate agency. Two chairs would be a tight fit on the gallery. Next to it sat Mercer Mortuary, inhabiting, to all appearances, what had once been a church. Across the street, a convenience store, Manny's, with a single gas pump out front. A grill made from a fifty-gallon drum cut in half and hinged, legs welded on, stood to one side under the overhang. Then came a long stretch of wooden houses set among trees, several with turrets or wraparound galleries.

We pulled into the shell driveway of a tan two-story with dark brown roof and trim whose elaborate gingerbread made me remember a trip to the Ozarks my family took when I was ten or so and the jigsaw with which, a year or so later, my father duplicated the boomerang I'd mail-ordered. On the first throw it had crashed against the garage and broken; I was devastated. My father fished a scrap of wood from a box of same, laid the broken pieces on top and made a new one. He used that same saw, and the band saw next to it, to make much of the furniture in the sprawling room we called the den. This was back before he turned into a piece of furniture himself—leaving my sister to take care of the family.

There was also the smell of figs. As a child, four years old maybe (couldn't have been much more, since Mom was gone the next year), I'd fallen from a fig tree in which I was climbing, had the breath knocked from me, and staggered onto the back porch where I lay gasping. Mom swept from the house, apron over print dress, hands white with flour, crying Help him! My father took one look and knew what had happened. He'll be all right, just give him a moment. Looks kinda like a fish, doesn't he?

The door was answered by a man wearing, I swear (I'd never seen one before, outside of movies), a smoking jacket. Dapper indeed, even if upon closer inspection the jacket's felt proved to be worn smooth, the tie beneath to be spotted with historic fluids and foodstuff. And while the glass in his hand held milk rather than a martini, the effect was much the same.

Actually, I later learned, it wasn't milk but something called a milk punch compounded of bourbon, milk and sugar. Easy on the ulcers, he'd tell me.

"Bubba!" this apparition said, blinking at the light. "What an absolutely marvelous surprise!" Heavy stress on *marvelous,* tiptoe pauses before and after. "And you've brought friends!"

"How's it going, Billy?"

"Please do come in. Come in, come in. All of you."

Ushered into a lavender living room, we stood there like de-bused campers uncertain what was expected of us. Purple vases, cobalt pitchers and violet-hued glasses sat about. Still-life paintings featuring bowls of fruit and fresh game, in the classical style but obviously new, hung on two walls. Above a mauve leather couch, the massive photograph of an erect penis, blown up to such point and such graininess as to become almost abstract, took pride of place above a mauve leather couch. On the opposite wall hung a poster of women's vaginas, like exotic fruit.

"We have company?" a voice piped from above.

"Henry Lee. And friends."

"Oh." Disappointment audible in the voice.

"What can I get you all? Perhaps some champagne? Always

a couple bottles chilling in the fridge. One never knows who might drop by, what possibilities for celebration the day could bring. Or mimosas! We've a sack of some of the biggest, juiciest oranges you're likely to see. From last weekend's farmer's market on the square?"

"Billy, this is Sheriff Bates. Mr. Turner's a detective down from Memphis."

"Oh, I love Memphis."

"I know you do."

"Good to meet you, Billy," Lonnie said.

Our eyes met, Billy's and mine, and we shook hands. His was surprisingly warm, his grip firm.

"Coffee sounds good," Lonnie went on, "if it's not too much trouble. Little early for anything else, for me."

"We have that. Coffee. Out in the kitchen somewhere."

He'd set his milk punch on a polished ebony table just inside the door, African origin from the look of it, in order to embrace Sims. Now he looked longingly towards it. So far away. He went to the base of the stairs and called weakly upwards: "Help!"

"Be right down."

"Sit, sit," our host said. "We don't often get company."

Lonnie glanced at Sims, who nodded.

"Something I need to ask you, Mr. Sims."

"Actually it's Roark. Henry Lee and I had different fathers. But please call me Billy."

"Billy, then. You used to direct movies, right?"

"That was a long time ago. All the sweet silly birds of our youth, surely they've flown by now. Mine have, at any rate. Yours?"

Lonnie smiled. "Occasionally they still come home to

roost. When they do, I try to make sure they get fed."

"Good for you. Speaking of which: I haven't served you all yet, have I? I really should attend to that." After gazing out the window for a moment, he went on. "It was a much smaller world back then. Everything was simpler. You had this feeling anything was possible—anything at all. I think I fancied myself a modern Shakespeare, half-owner of the Globe and running it, directing and acting in the very plays I wrote. I could do it all, create my *own* world. Create and inhabit it."

"He hasn't seen or thought of those movies in years. They have nothing to do with who he is now. You should not be bringing this in here, into our home. You know that, Henry."

All our heads turned to the source of the voice.

Sammy Cash stood at the foot of the stairs.

# Chapter Thirty-Five

HE WORE LOOSE KHAKI SLACKS, a pink oxford-cloth shirt from which the left collar button was missing, oxblood loafers, possibly Italian, without socks.

"Billy's offered refreshments, I assume?"

"He did. But then he kind of got off track."

"He does that. I won't say it's good to see you, Henry, it never is. Who are these people you've brought?"

"I'm the sheriff who answers to Henry Lee," Lonnie said. "Mr. Turner here is a consultant, helping me with an investigation. No reason you'd know this, but someone's driven murder right up on our steps and parked it there."

"In which case you should be off doing your job."

Lonnie glanced down at sockless feet, up to the missing button.

"I appreciate the fact this is your home, sir," he said, "and that I'm an intruder here."

Cash nodded.

"What *you* have to appreciate is that this is a murder investigation. Statutes give me a lot of latitude. Take me about eight seconds flat, for instance, to have you down on that polished wood floor in cuffs."

"Lonnie, surely—"

"You shut the fuck up too, Henry. Obstruction of justice's a big door. Don't make me open it."

"Oh dear," Billy said.

Lonnie sat beside him on the mauve couch. He'd snagged the milk punch on the way, and handed it to him. "I agree completely. Now." He looked from face to face. Mayor Sims, Billy Roark, the man we only knew as Sammy Cash. "Who's going to tell me what happened?"

★ ★ ★

BILLY ROARK WAS FOURTEEN YEARS OLDER than Henry Lee, out of the house and gone by the time Henry Lee was coming up, but always a role model—for that very reason if for no other. Because he'd reached escape velocity, you see, escaped the drag of the town they'd both grown up in, left behind the broken, near-mute mother and the fathers, gentle but long absent in Billy's case, violent in Henry Lee's. Billy Roark had gone up to Memphis at age nineteen and bluffed his way into selling furniture at Lowenstein's. Third day on the job he sold a houseful of it, a whole goddamn houseful, prime quality all, to an older, balding man and a magnificently stacked young blond. A runner was sent to the bank with the check and came back to report it was good. "I could use a man like you," the customer told him. A week later Billy found himself in a bright red Fairlane, coursing between El Paso and Dallas, flogging movies to drive-ins and main-street theaters with names like Malco and Paramount. He was a natural, able to turn on a dime, become whatever the customer seemed to expect of him. Theatre owners loved him and took whatever he had to offer. Soon a Cadillac replaced the Fairlane—a used Cadillac, and one day in of all places Fate, Texas, Pop. 1400, it broke down. Not much to do in Fate. He had breakfast at Mindy's Diner, lunch there a few hours later. Then he found himself at the Palace watching a film about a woman's prison. Jesus, he thought, this is what I've been selling? It was awful. He sat there watching, running numbers in his head. Obviously he was at the wrong end of the business. By six p.m., when he drove out of Fate with a new distributor cap and fuel pump, into a blood-red sunset, he'd blocked out what he was going to do. He found a place he could rent cameras, lights, the whole works, then some kids at a local college who'd been doing stage plays and figured how different could it be. Talked his current girlfriend, Sally Ann of the dirigible, gravity-defying breasts, into starring. Then over a weekend in a motel in New Braunfels, cartons of cigarettes, bags of hamburgers and bottles of Scotch ever to hand, not to mention Sally Ann, he roughed out a script. *Devil Women of Mars.* And it had, by God, everything. Scenes of small-town American life. Long shots of empty Arizona sky. Suspense. A message. Cleavage. Butts pushed up intriguingly by high-heel silver boots. When Billy drove out of New Braunfels that Monday, hungover in a borrowed car since he'd sold the Cad to get money for equipment rental, Sally Ann snoozing beside him, he was a new man. Everyone on his route, El Paso, Las Cruces, Midland-Odessa, Midlothian, Cockrel Hill, Duncanville, signed up for *Devil Women of Mars.* That next weekend, in an abandoned aircraft hangar outside Fort Worth, they shot the thing.

"It holds up, even now," Sammy Cash said. "I'm the guy who fills the gas tank when the kids pull into the Spur station. I see this thing in the back of the pickup and start backing away. Audience never sees it, all they have to go on is my reaction. The gas nozzle falls out. One of the kids goes to light a cigarette. I was in the first one he made, I was in the last one. He *is* a genius, you know."

Billy started cranking them out like no one had seen. He'd take a motel room for the weekend and emerge with a script, shoot the thing Monday through Wednesday, edit it that night and the next day, have it to the processors by late Thursday, out in the world the following week. Science fiction, horror, crime movies, prison films, teen exploitation. Sally Ann never appeared onscreen, nor remained long in Billy's life, after *Devil Women of Mars.* Most of the actors were amateurs, lured away from college and community-theatre productions or from porn films for a day or two, Sammy Cash (real name Gordie Ratliff) being the exception. He'd had small parts in several low-end Hollywood movies and proudly carried a Screen Actors Guild card. But when the guild found out he'd appeared in a nonunion film and busted him, he decided right then and there that their gentlemen's agreement was over. Never paid the fine, never looked back. And never again used any other name than Sammy Cash.

"It was as though the experience liberated him," Billy Roark said. "Before, he'd been a good journeyman, always dependable, you knew he'd show up on time, stay however long he was needed, get the job done. But then Sammy just … flowered. Soon *everyone* wanted him. Film after film—all of my own, those of half a dozen other filmmakers as well—he was brilliant, stone brilliant. Whatever the part."

All but imperceptibly at first, though, things began changing. TV became a six-hundred-pound linebacker flattening the opposition, providing, free and in one's own home, what B and lesser movies could provide only cheaply. Locally owned movie houses disappeared or were bought up by chains who in turn found themselves forced to bid high on upcoming Hollywood product and then, scrambling to meet expenses, to block bookings in every possible theatre. Meanwhile, costs of film, equipment rental and essential facilities such as editing studios increased astronomically. A few filmmakers held on. Till the bitter end.

★ ★ ★

"AND BY OUR TOENAILS," Billy Roark said. "Those days won't ever come again." He looked up. "Did we ever get you drinks? No? We really should do that. I'm afraid we're a bit out of practice vis-à-vis entertaining."

"He doesn't like to talk about all that," Sammy Cash said. "Rarely thinks much about it anymore."

The sadness in his companion's eyes belied him even before Billy spoke.

"I hated them for taking it all away from me. Taking away my life, really."

"Billy. Please," Sammy Cash said.

"There was talk about *The Giving* being my swan song, some kind of ultimate homage to the great art of film. Piss on that. What I was *giving* them, all of them—Hollywood, the studios, newcomer merchants who went about buying up everything in sight—was the finger. Fuckers didn't even have enough sense to know it. Swallow this, I was telling them.

Take this wad of crap and stuff it right back up where it came from."

"It's all right, Billy. All that's long in the past. We're fine now, aren't we? We have a good life." Sammy Cash looked from Lonnie's face to mine. "Don't you think you've upset him enough?"

"We never liked one another much, Gordie," Henry Lee said, "and you probably don't believe this, but I've always appreciated what you've done for my brother, your devotion to him."

Then, turning to Lonnie and me: "After Billy's troubles—"

"Troubles?" I said.

"A breakdown. He was in the hospital for almost a year. When he came out, I bought this house for him, set everything up so he'd be safe the rest of his life, never want for anything."

"Your brother cares for you a lot," the sheriff said. "So does Sammy."

Billy nodded.

"Did you ever meet a man by the name of Carl Hazelwood, Billy?" I asked.

No response this time. I thought of all those movies about submarines cutting engines and playing dead, hoping to stay off sonar.

"He'd been trying to get in touch with you. Carl's a great fan of yours, Billy. Maybe your *top* fan. He understood what you were doing, what you'd accomplished. He wanted desperately to talk to you about the films you made, tell you how important they'd been to him."

"I—" Billy began. Even the drink was dry when he tried for refuge there. Foundering, lost, he looked about. At

Sammy's face. Out the window. At these familiar walls.

"Others did everything they could to keep him away from you, Billy. But he wasn't going to be stopped. It was that important to him. *You* were that important to him."

Lonnie's gaze turned to Henry Lee.

"You knew about this all along."

He nodded. "Boy showed up at my door one night. Hadn't bathed for a month or two. Mumbling and twitching. Said he was looking for the man who'd made *The Giving*. What was I supposed to do? What would *you* do? I had to protect Billy. I told him—Carl Hazelwood, as we later learned—that I didn't know any such person. Told him to go away. Okay, sorry to have bothered you, sir, he said. But he didn't go away. Far from it. I'd catch glimpses of him scuttling behind the garage, slipping off into the woods."

"He'd seen more than enough movies to know about stakeouts," Lonnie said. "And despite your disavowals, he knew you were connected with Billy, if not precisely what the relationship was. Knew he had only to keep watch."

"And go through my mail."

"That's how he found his way to Billy."

"Enough," Sammy Cash said. "*Enough,* goddamn it."

"Did you talk to Carl Hazelwood, Billy?"

His eyes wandered about, settled on Sammy, who shook his head. Billy nodded. "Nice young man."

"Yes. Yes, he was."

"Told me people were still watching my films, still talking about them. I had no idea. He only came that one time. I asked him to dinner the next night, insisted on cooking, though Sammy usually does all that. Baked bass, a salad of couscous and goat cheese. Put out the good china, chilled two bottles of white. We waited almost two hours, but he never showed."

Billy's eyes came up and went from face to face.

"Sammy—"

"I'm sorry," Sammy Cash said. He held a handgun. "This has to be over now. Billy's suffered enough."

"What you have there's a twenty-two," Lonnie said. "Shoot someone with that, you're likely to make them mad." He stood and, hand extended, stepped forward. The gun barked. Bubbles of blood spotted his lips.

"Son of a *bitch*," Lonnie said.

# Chapter Thirty-Six

THE SECOND SHOT HAD STRUCK Billy square in the neck—transecting his trachea, though we didn't know that at the time. I don't think Sammy Cash even intended to fire. When he saw what he'd done, not knowing even the half of it, his hand fell onto his lap and he sat immobile, tears in his eyes like chandeliers in empty ballrooms. For the moment Lonnie seemed okay: down but not out. I'd pulled Billy from the chair onto the floor, felt for a carotid. Thinking with amazement how much blood a body holds, how much blood it gives up, and how quickly. Billy wasn't breathing. Pinching his nose, hyperextending his neck, I stacked in three quick breaths and checked again. Still no pulse, no respiration. I began compressions. When next I looked up, Lonnie had been there by me, counting. He'd do the breaths, turn aside to spit blood or cough as I did compressions. Three, four minutes in, he folded, gasping. That's when I put the mayor to work. Need your help over here, I said. Now.

A middle-aged man in badly faded purple scrubs walked through automatic doors into the waiting room and spoke briefly with the volunteer at the desk before coming towards me. "Mr. Turner?" Fatigue sat heavily in his eyes. "You're with Sheriff Bates, right?"

I nodded.

"He's going to be okay. The bullet barely nicked an upper lobe. Of his lung, that is. Simple enough to deal with. Blood loss, shock to the system, that's a different thing, that's what's on the boards now. Take some time for full recovery, I'm afraid."

"And Billy Roark?"

"The other GSW? What, you're with him, too?"

"I've been working with Sheriff Bates on a murder case. It's all connected."

"I see..." He looked at the window, at a gurney being pushed along the hallway upon which lay an oxygen tank, electronic monitors, IV pumps and the deformed body of a young girl, then back at me. "Mr. Roark expired over an hour ago." He told me about the trachea, *just like you'd hack a garden hose in two,* how, despite our best efforts at the scene, Roark had gone too long without oxygen. His heart stopped twice in ER. The second time, they failed to restart it. "I'm sorry. We did everything we could."

★ ★ ★

"STRANGE AS IT MAY SEEM LOOKING about that house, the way Bill and Sammy were together, they were only partners. Close partners, but never lovers. Sometimes it was almost as though they were a single being. For years. How can things come apart so quickly?"

"I'm sorry, Mayor."

"Lonnie's going to be all right, they say."

"He'll be out of commission for a while. Back on the job soon enough."

"Good. That's good. I should have spoken up. I didn't know. I suspected. Most of all—"

"Most of all you hoped your brother hadn't done it."

"I didn't want to lose him."

"I understand."

"Or for him to lose himself again—which is more or less what happened that other time. Before he went to the hospital, I mean. He seemed fine. A little quiet. Then he just … floated away. He'd always been a dynamo, five or six projects going at once. The breakdown, or the drugs, or the electroshock, they changed him. He came back. But he'd become this meek, sweet man—the one you met."

*All that he said, about his movie giving them the finger,* Sammy Cash told me. *That wasn't true. He was trying to make a good movie. In his mind, I think, a great movie. Something he'd be remembered for. After years of churning them out, ambition,* real *ambition, had overtaken him.*

*Did he succeed?*

*Hard to say. All we know for sure is that he never made another one—because he did exactly what he wanted with that one, or because he realized that really was the best he could do? Ambition is a strange rider. Sometimes the horse it picks can't carry it.*

*Our house?* he suddenly said.

*Yes.*

*The decorating's mine. Everything else in our life is Billy. You have no idea how much I did for him. Everything. He was so sweet… That man, Hazelwood, should never have come. After he left, Billy was agitated. There's nothing to stop me, he kept saying over and over, I could go back, I could work again. The look in his eye was a terrible thing. Hazelwood had told me where he was staying. I went there and tried to talk to him. Told him if he truly cared about Billy he'd leave him alone, but he wouldn't listen. What else could I do? I had to stop him. I couldn't let Billy be hurt again. And now ... Now I've made Billy immortal, just a little, haven't I? No one will ever forget how Hazelwood died. And whenever they think of that, they'll remember Billy's movie.*

He was quiet for a while.

*It's harder than you think to kill a man.*

I nodded, remembering.

*They don't die easy.* He looked up. *You have to keep on killing them.*

★ ★ ★

I REMEMBER LYING ON MY BUNK back in prison waiting to die. Definitely I wasn't one of the bad ol' boys. From the first there'd been verbal baiting, buckets of attitude, people stepping up to me, sudden explosions of violence, broken noses, broken limbs. Everyone inside knew I was a cop. So I just naturally expected the next footsteps I heard would be coming for me.

One night a few weeks in, I heard them slapping down the tier, footsteps that is, figuring this was it. Nothing happened, though, and after a time I realized that what I was hearing, what I was waiting for, wasn't footsteps at all, it was only rain. I started laughing.

A voice came from the next cell. "New Meat?"

"Yeah."

"You lost it over there?"

Half an hour past lights out. From the darkness around us

were delivered discrete packets of sound: snoring, farts, grunts clearly sexual in nature, toilets flushing. A single bulb burned at the end of each tier. Guards' steel-toed boots rang on metal stairs and catwalks.

"Damn if I don't think I have," I told him.

# Chapter Thirty-Seven

LOSING IT'S THE KEY, THE SECRET no one tells you. From the first day of your life, things start piling up around you: needs, desires, fears, dependencies, regrets, lost connections. They're always there. But you can decide what to do with them. Polish them and put them up on the shelf. Stack them out behind the house by the weeping willow. Haul them out on the front porch and sit on them.

The front porch is where Val and I were. She had on jeans, a pink T-shirt, hair tied up in a matching pink bandanna. I was thinking how it had all started with Lonnie Bates and myself out here on the porch just like this. Where Lonnie's Jeep had been then, Val's yellow Volvo sat. That seemed long ago now.

Val and I were both playing hooky. Somehow the world, our small corner of it, would survive such irresponsibility.

"All our conflicts, even the most physical of them, the most petty—at the center they're moral struggles," Val said.

"I don't know. We like to think that. It gives us comfort. Just as we want to believe, need to believe, that our actions come from elevated motives. From principles. When in truth they only derive from what our characters, what our personal and collective histories, dictate. We're ridden by those histories, the same way voodoo spirits inhabit living bodies, which they call horses."

"People can change. Look at yourself."

There's change and there's change, of course. The city council had tried to hire me as acting sheriff and I'd said you fools have the wrong man. Now, *just till Lonnie returns, we all understand that, right?,* I was working as deputy under Don Lee. I'd come here to excuse myself, to further what I perceived as exemption, to withdraw from humanity. Instead I'd found myself rejoining it.

Val a case in point.

"I have something for you," I told her. I went in and brought it out. She opened the battered, worn case. The instrument inside by contrast in fine shape. Inlays of stars, a crescent moon, real ivory as pegheads.

"It's—"

"I know what it is. A Whyte Laydie. They're legendary. I've never actually seen one before, only pictures."

"It was my father's. His father's before him. I'd like you to have it."

She ticked a finger along the strings. "You never told me he played."

"He didn't, by the time I came along. But he had."

"You can't just up and give something like this away, Turner."

"It's my way of saying I hope you'll both stay close to me."

The banjo and Val, or my father and Val? She didn't ask. With immense care, she took the instrument from its case, placed it in her lap, began tuning. "This is amazing. I don't know what to say."

The fingernail of her second finger, striking down, sounded the third string, brushed across, then dropped to the fourth for a hammer-on. Between, in that weird syncopation heard nowhere else, her cocked thumb sounded the fifth.

> *Li'l Birdie, L'il Birdie,*
> *Come sing to me a song.*
> *I've a short while to be here*
> *And a long time to be gone.*

Val held the banjo out before her, looking at it. I had forgotten, or maybe I never fully understood until that very moment, what a magnificent thing it was: a work of art in itself, a tool, an alternate tongue, blank canvas, an entire waiting and long-past world. Lovingly, reverentially, Val set it back in its case. "I don't deserve this. I'm not sure anyone deserves this."

"Instruments should be played. Just as lives should be lived."

She nodded.

"Come with me."

"Where?"

"A special place."

Off the porch and fifty steps along, the woods closed around us, we'd left civilization behind. Trees towered above. Undergrowth teemed with bustling, unseen things. Even sunlight touched down gingerly here. We paced alongside a stream, came suddenly onto a small lake filled with cypress.

There were perhaps two dozen trees. Hundreds of knees breaking from the surface. Steam drifted, an alternate, otherworldly atmosphere, on the water.

"I grew up next to a place just like this."

"You've never told me much about your childhood."

"No. But I will."

I reached for her hand.

"I spoke to my sister this morning. The one who raised me. I was thinking about going to see her, wondered if you might consider coming with me."

"Arizona? Be a little like visiting Oz. I've always been curious about Oz."

"My grandfather—the one who owned the banjo? His name was John Cleveland. He spent much of his life wading among cypress like this. Made things from the knees. Bookends, coffee tables, lamps. Most of my favorite books I first read in the shade of a lamp he'd made for me. He'd carved faces on the knees, like a miniature Mount Rushmore, even drilled out holes so I could keep pencils there. He'd come back from the lake and head straight for the workshop, stand there with his pants dripping wet because he'd come across a new knee that suggested something to him. Walk into that workshop, all you'd see was half an acre of cypress knees. Like being here, without the water."

"It's all but unbearably beautiful, isn't it?" Val said. "I feel as though I'm standing witness to creation." Her arm came around my waist, heat of her body mixing with my own. "Thank you."

Shot with sunlight, the mist was dispersing. A crane kited in over the trees, dipped to skim the water and went again aloft.

Speechless, we watched. Sunlight skipped bright disks of gold off the water.

"Guess we should get to work, huh?"

"Soon," Val said. "Soon."

# ORDER THE COMPLETE JAMES SALLIS COLLECTION

| | | |
|---|---|---|
| **Driven** *(new title)* | 978-184243-837-4 | £7.99 |
| The Long-Legged Fly | 978-184243-696-7 | £9.99 |
| Moth | 978-184243-700-1 | £9.99 |
| Black Hornet | 978-184243-704-9 | £9.99 |
| Eye of the Cricket | 978-184243-708-7 | £9.99 |
| Bluebottle | 978-184243-712-4 | £9.99 |
| Ghost of a Flea | 978-184243-716-2 | £9.99 |
| Cypress Grove | 978-184243-728-5 | £9.99 |
| Cripple Creek | 978-184243-732-2 | £9.99 |
| Salt River | 978-184243-736-0 | £9.99 |
| Drive | 978-184243-724-7 | £9.99 |
| The Killer is Dying | 978-184243-740-7 | £9.99 |
| Death Will Have Your Eyes | 978-184243-720-9 | £9.99 |

**Limited Edition Boxed Set    978-184243-886-2      £99**
(Only 100 sets available containing all thirteen titles including *Driven*.
Plus a FREE twelve inch vinyl of James Sallis music and two short
stories specially recorded for this publication.)

## Order online at www.noexit.co.uk/Sallis

Name:

Address:


Date:                    Order Number:            Credit Card Number:

Expiry Date:          Issue Number:            Security Code (3 digit):

*NO EXIT PRESS*, PO Box 394, Harpenden, AL5 1XJ, U.K.
Tel: 01582 766348 or 020 7430 1021.
Free postage & packing in the UK, £10 for Euroland
and £20 for the Rest of the World.
For single copy orders £3.95 for Euroland
and £6.95 for the Rest of theWorld
(Cheques in £Sterling drawn on UK bank payable to
Oldcastle Books Ltd)